PRAISE FOR JAIMIE ENGLE

Kirkus Editor's Choice 2020
L. Ron Hubbard Writers of the Future Award
Sunshine State & Land of Enchantment Book List contender
Quarterfinalist Publisher's Weekly Book Life Prize Non-Fiction
Publisher's Weekly Book Life Prize Fiction
Top Ten Book of the year Kid Lit Reviews

"…the world Engle has created in this novel is an intriguing one, equal parts familiar and fantastic." *Kirkus Reviews*

"…belongs on your bookshelf - young or old - right along with Tolkien and Grimm." –5-Star Review

"I did not want to leave until the last page was turned." –Kid Lit Reviews

"…the same kind of universe you might meet Captain Malcolm Reynolds or Luke Skywalker in." –The Story Sanctuary Reviews

"…a dazzling, fresh plot." –5-Star Review

"A tale presents troubled adolescence and romance through the eyes of a remarkable teen protagonist." –Kirkus Editor's Choice & Review

"Metal Mouth is a brilliantly original tale that explores many concerns countless people deal with every day…" –Reader's Choice Review

"…a wry and wise romantic heartbreaker touched with mystery, lightning, and shivery hints of the supernatural." –Book Life Prize

"…explained and explored thoroughly… structure and development is very well executed" –Book Life Prize Non-Fiction

BOOKS BY JAIMIE ENGLE

FICTION

Clifton Chase and the Arrow of Light, Book 1
One boy is chosen to change history

Clifton Chase and the Arrow of Light, Coloring Book
Condensed version of the novel with pictures to color

Clifton Chase on Castle Rock, Book 2
The adventure continues, only this time it's with Robin Hood

Clifton Chase on Castle Rock, Coloring Book 2
Condensed version of book two with pictures to color

The Dredge
Supernatural gifts are sought through deception in a future world

Dreadlands: Wolf Moon
A Viking boy must face shifting wolves or become their prey

The Toilet Papers: Places to Go, While you Go
Short story collection of humor, horror, and historical for adults 16+

The Toilet Papers, Jr.
Short story collection of humor, horror, & fairy tales for kids 8-12

Metal Mouth
A girl's braces transmit a boy's voice after she's struck by lightning

NON-FICTION

Clifton Chase and the Arrow of Light Teacher Guide
Teacher Curriculum Guide to use with the novel

Write a Book that Doesn't Suck (Indie Series Book #2)
A No-Nonsense Guide to Writing Epic Fiction

How to Publish Your Book (Indie Series Book #1)
A step-by-step ebook to get your book published!

Visit the author at JaimieEngle.com

Clifton Chase
on
Castle Rock

Jaimie Engle

Book friends are best friends!

2021

JME Books

Edited by The Write Engle, LLC
The text for this book is set in Fairfield LT Std Light

Published in the United States by JME Books

Visit us on the Web: www.JaimieEngle.com

Educators and librarians, for an author visit
or bulk order discounts, email publicity@thewriteengle.com.

Summary: Clifton Chase loses the Arrows of Light and must travel back to the
eleventh century to help Robin Hood save the people.

ISBN: 978-1-7328786-7-9

Realistic Fiction that Questions Reality…
Where Everyday Kids Become Heroes!
JME Books

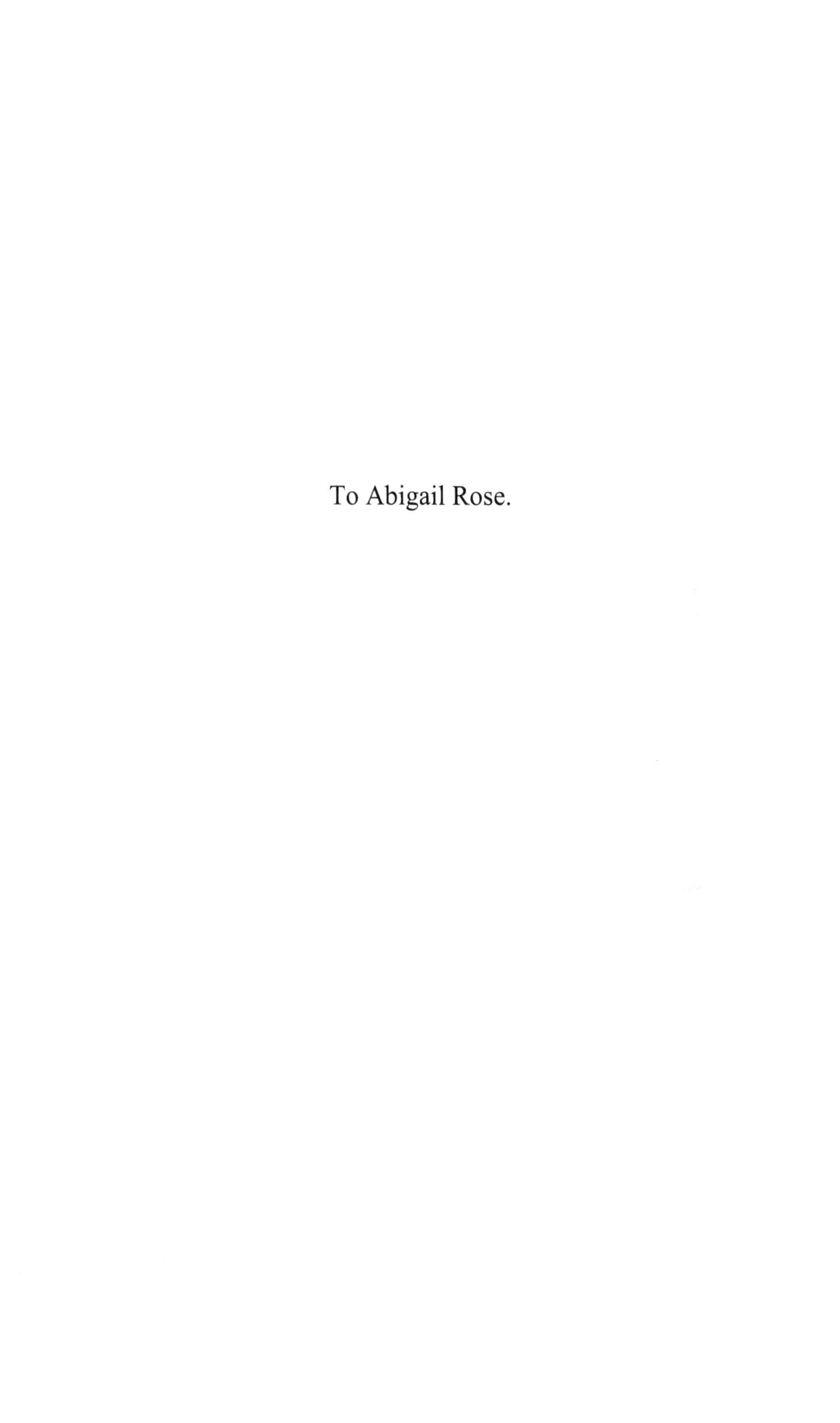

To Abigail Rose.

Part One:

The Boy

Book Two

Chapter One
Normal

There is no way of knowing, when the day begins like any other, that something extraordinary lies on the horizon. On a normal morning in a normal town, Clifton Chase opened his eyes. He had no reason to suspect anything out of the ordinary. No warning by woodland creature, no March wind whispering he remain vigilant on this particular day. In fact, it began in the same predictable manner as every other morning.

And Clifton was glad.

He dressed in jeans and a T-shirt that read **Rainault Plumbing: Our Pipes Hit the Mark** in big block letters. His stomach grumbled, a bloodhound sniffing for breakfast, and led him to the kitchen.

"Clifton," his mother called from her bedroom. "We're leaving for archery club in five minutes."

"That's today?" he called back.

"Yes, and we're running late."

Clifton scarfed down cereal, slurped milk, and placed his dish in the sink. Skidding in tube socks down the hardwood floor, he rushed into his bedroom. He liked his room. It was warm and comfortable with a stained oak bed, matching dresser, and end table. Over the years, he'd grown an impressive collection of medieval relics, from antique stores, estate sales, and by wealthy relatives vacationing in Europe. His two prize possessions were his lucky iron horseshoe lamp and a wooden plank with hilts and pommels screwed in for hanging his backpack and coats.

His closet door glided across the thick rug. Clifton reached for his sneakers but stopped. Beside the bookcase packed with boardgames and novels, wedged behind art supplies and science equipment, he spotted the copper feather, one that unquestionably took residence while he slept, as the space had been vacant when he tossed his sneakers in the night before.

He'd hidden the three arrows in the back of his closet, out of sight, out of mind. Beautifully crafted, the first arrow ushered him through time to 1485 England, where he'd rescued two princes from their tyrant uncle, fought in an epic battle, and witnessed his good friend, a dwarf named Dane, die before his eyes. Forced amnesia fed his denial of any adventure through time. A centuries old oil painting, depicting Clifton with the notched arrow on a battlefield, evidenced the proof that it had happened.

He passed his fingers through the barbs of the fletching, like the feathers from nesting birds that floated to his porch in the spring. Only these gleamed in a striking copper flecked with gold, shades he'd never seen on the wings of any Florida birds. The wood shaft, he remembered, was forged from the Tree of Knowledge, where Simurgh the all-knowing bird of reason nested before Time herself existed on Earth.

He knew these things, but he wanted to forget.

Except for Pearl, the beautiful Siren who rescued him from an evil Mer King. Her memory was locked away from the rest. Why, just the thought of Pearl and the lightweight shaft heated in his hand as the Arrow of Light brightened and the fletching shimmered.

Then a pair of glowing eyes, at the rear of the closet, shone like spotlights. Clifton blinked hard and shook his head. The eyes were gone. It had to be something else. He stepped closer. Something jutted out from between his coats like a witch's nose. He leaned in closer still. Was his jacket moving? Clifton took in a sharp breath.

Someone else was in his closet.

With all the bravery he could muster, Clifton reached a shaky hand toward the nose, relieved when he palmed the hard wood hanger instead. He smacked it and scolded himself for letting his fear paint such vivid pictures in his mind. As he stepped back, the Arrow of Light snagged on something that tugged it, nearly yanking it from his grip. Clifton twisted around and pulled hard, expecting a tug-of-war but getting no tension from whatever had held the arrow captive. His own force sent him sailing into a stack of boardgames, which toppled to the floor. Pieces flew across the rug and Clifton smacked the ground at the base of his bookshelf, now with no doubt in his mind that someone else was in his closet.

He jumped up, plunged back into darkness, and flung his clothes aside to find nothing but the wall. No escape into Narnia for Clifton. He ran his fingers through his hair. What was the matter with him? But he knew. The Arrows of Light held magic. Many beings would endure the impossible to unearth them for personal gain. No matter how desperately Clifton wished life would return to normal, as long as he possessed the arrows, it never would.

Then an eerie feeling, as if on cue, struck him, and he worried someone was tiptoeing behind him. Clifton jumped around half-expecting to catch the glowing-eyed monster, but instead found his mom in the doorway.

"What are you doing? It's time to go. Never mind, just…grab Grandpa Samuel's archery set if you want. You can try it out today on the field."

"Do I have to?"

Mom scoffed. "Seriously? I figured you'd be dying to shoot those arrows. Is something wrong with them? You haven't shot them once since Dad and I gave them to you."

"I know," Clifton said. "I just don't think I'm ready yet. They're really old, Mom."

"That's kind of the point," Mom's voice trailed. "We're late. Let's go!"

He was about to stash the arrow in the back of his closet with the other two, when he decided he'd place them all in his backpack for safekeeping. Just in case someone really *was* after them. He threw on shoes without tying the laces and deserted the room unable to see the creature in his closet, eclipsed in darkness.

Chapter Two
Nice Shot

Melbourne's Wickham Park was a nearly 400-acre county facility housing horse stalls, a dog park, and a modernized playground. Birds, like scrubs and egrets, perched on oak branches and squirrels scampered across the felled pine needles beneath. Catfish and snapping turtles made their home in the large lake at the park's center.

Clifton's mom crept across the windy road at a pace Clifton bet he could match on his bike if he pedaled hard enough. As they rode, he pointed out different species of birds and trees to his baby brother Pierce, who giggled and pointed out the window too. Mom smiled into the rearview mirror as she turned off the paved path onto a dirt road.

As they snaked down the narrow pass, Clifton imagined archers hidden behind the hedges that fanned out in even rows, ending at large wooden targets.

Carefully, he scanned for the King's men awaiting their command to fire on his pretend chariot. At the last row, he did a double take, when he swore the same pair of glowing eyes from his closet peered at him through the bushes.

The road opened to a large field lined with parked cars, where amateur archers reacquainted at the monthly Saturday class. Mom parked. She unbuckled Pierce from his car seat and scooted to the trunk for his bag of dump trucks, shovels, and pails.

Clifton ambled over carrying his pack. "Do you need help, Mom?"

"No. You go on," she said. "I've got this."

Clifton jogged to a group of boys fencing with foam covered PVC pipes wrapped in duct tape. "Hey, guys," Clifton said.

"Hey, bro," Juan said, his brown eyes magnified behind thick glasses.

The last time Clifton saw Juan, they were foraging for arrows in *The Hinterland*, the open field behind the targets where poorly shot arrows rested. Clifton had found the Arrow of Light wedged in a tree stump, and when he touched it, magic transported him into the past.

He shivered at the memory.

The identical twins Matt and Max engaged in a duel equaled only by Obi Wan and Anakin at the end of Episode Three. Matt jabbed at Max's gut and Max leapt, barely missing the sword's blunt tip. Though the tape wrapped swords were not sharp, Clifton would find bright red welts on his arms and legs afterwards.

"Pretty boring fight," Ava said from a high tree branch, her blonde hair in a loose ponytail.

“Yeah,” echoed Julia seated beside her.

“That’s easy to say from up there,” Max said, swinging his sword in the air.

Without hesitating, Ava swung to a low branch then dropped to the ground. She adjusted her stance for battle-pose and held her sword. “Now, how about a real matchup?”

Max mirrored her stance. “If you think you can handle it.”

The two clashed swords and Clifton laughed as Ava fenced Max closer and closer to the surrounding woods, now more like Rey verses Kylo Ren. Julia glared and Clifton stopped laughing. The warm sun and cool, spring breeze blowing off the Atlantic coast made it a perfect day.

A perfectly, ordinary day.

“Archers!” a voice boomed out.

The large group of boys and girls assembled quickly around the heavyset man’s opened hatchback. He sat on the bed. Hefty legs hung over the bumper, and Clifton could swear the metal hinges gasped as they supported his weight.

“My name is Mr. Anderson. I am a volunteer instructor in basic archery.” Clifton smiled. He liked how seriously the old man took archery club. “How many of you have never shot an arrow before?”

Several hands shot up, kids ranging in age from six to sixteen.

“All right,” Mr. Anderson said. “Those of you familiar with shooting an arrow will please take notice of those who may be in need of your assistance.”

Clifton surveyed the new faces. He noticed Ryan Rivales and looked away before they could make eye contact. Antagonistic and arrogant, he was a bomb with a short fuse and although Clifton offered an apology, Ryan refused it. He squirmed, his focus on Mr. Anderson waning, drawn instead to the car pulling into the parking area. It was his best friend, Justin, who grabbed a black compound bow and quiver out of the car and ran over. Clifton waved, and as he turned back to the group, Ryan was staring at him.

Clifton pretended not to care, attentive to Mr. Anderson until he climbed off the tailgate. The hinges sighed with relief. The group broke out into their assigned stations, with newcomers lining up to shoot first.

"Hey, Clifton. Did I miss anything?" Justin asked, making a beeline to the field.

"Just the same old instructions we get every month. Oh, and Ava out-fenced Max. It was savage."

"Seriously? Man, I can't believe I missed that," Justin said, his blue eyes widening.

"Won't be the last time, that's for sure."

The shooting range, covered with targets nailed to wooden posts, ended at brush-covered sand dunes. With the range "cold," archers searched *The Hinterland* for stray arrows that had missed their targets.

"It's simple, really," Clifton overheard Ryan tell the twins. "Bows use elastic potential energy from your arm and convert it into kinetic energy to the arrow. It's just a transfer, like time or food or the force of a fist."

Ryan slugged Matt in the arm and the twin teetered.

"What's your problem?" Max asked.

"I don't have a problem. I'm helping you *tryhards* understand how archery works. You should be thanking me." He crossed to where Clifton and Ryan stood. "What a waste it is to hoard energy from a thing that wants to be used, to be shot through the air…like an arrow."

"Let's go, Justin." Clifton remained neutral, the Switzerland of Wickham Park archery club. No involvement, no matter how badly Ryan taunted him. The last time he'd given him headspace, they'd fought in the gym and Clifton got suspended, grounded, and forced to write two apology letters, one of which was to Ryan.

Never again, he thought.

Justin didn't budge. Ava and Julia ran over to check on Matt. "What's your deal?" Ava said to Ryan, arms crossed at her chest.

A smile wormed across Ryan's face. "Well, hello, Ava. It's good to see you. Are you ready to dump these tryhards and hang out with me?"

Ava grimaced. "Why do you have to be so mean? Just leave my friends alone."

Ryan faced Matt. "You need a girl to fight for you? That's pathetic." Ryan shoved him and Matt turned to walk away. "That's it, isn't it?" He shoved harder, nearly knocking him to the ground.

Clifton looked away, flight or fight kicking in as adrenaline muddled his mind. No, this wasn't his fight and he should leave before someone dragged him in. Too late. He caught Ava's gorgeous eyes pleading with him to do something, to do anything.

He did nothing.

Fueled by an anger Clifton assumed he'd ignited, Ava stepped between Ryan and Matt. "Why don't you back off, jerk," she said. "Pick on someone your own size."

"Who, like Chase?" Clifton's fists balled at the mention of his name. "Nah. Chase is too much of a squeaker. He only stands up to me when there's a teacher around to get him out of it. Ain't that right, Chase?"

Clifton held his gaze for a moment before averting his attention to the ground. He wouldn't be drawn into a battle that wasn't his to fight ever again. Even if Ava's glare penetrated, her disappointment jagged.

Ryan shook his head. "Just like I thought." He faced Ava. "You're wasting your time with him. He's a nobody."

Ava didn't defend Clifton. No one did. Max and Matt stood helplessly on the field as Ryan and his goons went back to the line, cutting to the front. Clifton knew he should've done more. He should've stood up to Ryan and defended the twins. Instead, Ava was the only one speaking out for all of them. But Ryan could be so frustrating, and he knew exactly how to push Clifton's buttons. Like when he said Clifton only stood up to him if a teacher was around. That wasn't true. Ryan was the squeaker, not him.

Suddenly, he didn't want to be at archery club anymore, couldn't stand the way Ava and the twins stared at him. He wanted to say something, say anything, but he couldn't. Instead, he silently turned and plodded back to his mom's van, knowing with each step, life grew less and less normal.

Chapter Three
Home

"Hey, Clifton, wait up!" Justin jogged beside him. "Where're you going?"

"Home."

"Home? But I just got here. What's wrong?"

"I don't want to talk about it." Clifton marched ahead, with Justin a morning shadow.

"Clifton, stop, man. C'mon."

Reluctantly, Clifton stalled in his tracks. "What, dude?"

"What's up with you? You're acting weird lately, and not only today."

"That's why you made me stop? To tell me what's wrong with me? Thanks a lot."

Clifton hit the gas, but Justin grabbed his arm. "You know what I mean. We've been friends since second grade. I know you, man. And I know when something's bothering you that you don't wanna talk about."

Clifton glared. "Then if you know I'm not gonna talk about it, why are you bothering?"

"Cause we're best friends. That's what best friends do."

Clifton didn't feel like anyone's friend. He'd let Ava defend the twins, stayed silent when Ryan accused him of being a squeaker, and now he was choosing to hide secrets from his best friend in the whole world, all because of a stupid magic arrow. But just the thought of having that conversation twisted his stomach. Would he believe Justin if the roles were reversed? Probably not.

"We are, aren't we?" Justin said, interrupting his inner dialogue.

"Are what?"

"Best friends."

"Of course, we're best friends. You know that."

Justin shifted his weight, his point made.

Clifton swatted at the air. "I don't know. It's like, I'm screwing everything up, you know? And I don't think there's anything I can do to fix it."

Justin nodded. "Well, as my Uncle Rob always says, the painter can't fix the dishwasher."

Fanning out his hands, Clifton said, "What in the world is that supposed to mean?"

Justin shrugged. "I don't know. Like, maybe you're not the only person supposed to fix everything all the time. Maybe if you didn't try to do it all yourself and you actually asked for help from your friends once in a while, you wouldn't feel this way."

If Justin only knew.

"Do me a favor?" Clifton asked. "Tell Ava I said good-bye. I think she's mad at me."

"All right, man," Justin said with a handshake they'd made up in the fourth grade. "See you at school Monday."

Clifton crossed the field to the picnic table near his mom's van, where Pierce played with a toy truck and Mom talked with a parent. He knelt beside his brother. "Whatchya doing, buddy?"

"Playing with my truck."

"That's cool. Can I play too?"

"Okay."

Pierce handed over the toy construction truck and Clifton ran it back and forth in the sand, making engine noises with his lips. Pierce laughed. No matter what was wrong in the world, his baby brother reminded him that life was simple. Joy was a choice. Peace, a commodity. Friendship, a privilege. In his power, was the ability to make things right if he were brave enough to take the chance.

Clifton handed back the truck. "Thanks for sharing."

The dry snap of a branch in the wooded area separating the pavilion from the lake stole his attention. Clifton swung around and scanned the trees. Greens and browns, textured wood, and smooth leaf, caught in a net of shadows. He thought he saw a form, but the harder he stared the fuzzier the spot grew.

"Clifton," his mom said. "What are you doing over here? It doesn't look like club's over yet."

"I'm really not feeling it today, Mom. I kinda wanna go home."

Mom placed her hands on her hips. “Did something happen? Did that Ryan boy bother you again?”

“No, Mom. Jeez. Can't a guy just wanna go home? Is that a crime?”

“Okay, okay. I'm just asking a simple question,” Mom said, her hands lifted in surrender. “But your defensive answers lead me to believe you're not telling me the truth.”

Clifton rolled his eyes, stood, and stomped away. Why did everyone keep telling him he was hiding something? So what, if he was. They weren’t supposed to know. Should he blurt out to his mom how he was struggling to deal with the Battle of Bosworth Field, where he had killed King Richard III? She would freak out and never leave him alone again, not even to use the bathroom. And the same was true of Justin and Ava. They acted like they wanted to know what was going on, but if he told them he rode on the back of a mythical creature named Simurgh, into and out of the 15th century, they would never speak to him again.

No one would.

“I wanna go home,” Clifton called back to his mom.

Pierce wrapped tiny arms around Clifton’s waist. Clifton sat him in his car seat, snapped the buckles, and handed him his sippy cup, before circling the car to sit beside him. He stared out the window as Mom packed up her things and said good-bye.

After several minutes, Mom sat in the driver’s seat, clicked her seatbelt, and said, “You're positive you don't want to stay?” Clifton's are-you-serious face gave her the answer. “Okay,” she said as she put the car in drive. “Looks like rain anyway.”

They were quiet, with the lull of the engine rocking Pierce to sleep, and Clifton not too far behind. He stared at the dark sky. The rain threatened to burst open the clouds. As Mom pulled into the garage, large raindrops landed on the walk and thunder clapped. Clifton grabbed the diaper bag while Mom carried Pierce inside, and the thunderheads released their downpour. The cranking garage door closing behind him was the roar of a prehistoric monster.

Somedays, the world looks different if you let it, and as he stepped inside his house, Clifton took in his surroundings. The living room couches were worn, yet comfortable. The kitchen table held meals filled with memories. He loved his house and his family, but ever since he’d returned from his adventure through time, he felt like an outsider. It was hard to feel like part of the family when he was keeping secrets from his parents.

His mom knocked on his bedroom door and pushed it opened. “Pierce is sleeping in his bed. I’m exhausted. I think I'm going to take a nap too. Are you okay alone? Do you mind?”

“Of course, I don't mind, Mom. Go to sleep.”

“Okay, sweetie. Wake me up if you need anything.” She closed the door and Clifton listened to her footfalls soften as she padded down the hall.

He flopped down on his bed. What was the matter with him? The Arrow of Light had chosen Clifton for a reason and he'd fulfilled that purpose, so why did everything still feel off? He wondered if he was going crazy or something. As the rain fell in a steady stream against his bedroom window, he closed his eyes, hoping that when he opened them again, everything would be unremarkable. But no matter how badly he wanted his run-of-the-mill life, the three glowing arrows in his backpack precluded normalcy.

Chapter Four
Grandpa Samuel

The scent of baking chicken carried through the house and opened Clifton's eyes. He heard his dad's voice and sighed. Not only had he fallen asleep, but Mom woke up first, which meant she'd already told Dad about what had happened at Archery Club. He sat up and hung his legs over the mattress edge. He'd wanted to head Dad off to explain his point of view. It was crucial he struck first, before Mom had her chance to blurt out how Clifton had refused to stay, then stomped off to the car, *blah, blah, blah*. But he'd messed up everything.

Dad was a big believer in only two types of commitment. You were either in or out. When Clifton was younger, he had wanted to become a hockey player. He went to one practice, got knocked in the shins by a stick, and never went back. Dad gave him a pass. Then, when Clifton wanted to play the guitar and start a rock band, he was forced to endure six months of lessons, even though after six weeks if was apparent he possessed zero talent for music.

Reluctantly, Clifton opened his door and went to the kitchen, yawning as he stepped in.

“Hey, buddy,” Dad said. “How was your day?”

Mom was setting the table as Dad poured himself a tall glass of milk.

“Okay,” Clifton said, giving them both sidelong glances. Maybe Mom hadn't said anything yet.

“Your mom said you left Archery Club early today. You want to talk about it?”

His shoulders slumped. The cat was out. “Nothing to talk about, really,” Clifton said. “I just wasn't feeling it today.”

“Oh…you weren't *feeling* it, huh?” Dad set down his milk and took a seat. “You know what I love to do, Clifton?” Dad asked, and Clifton knew Dad was about to give a lecture, not actually expecting an answer to his question. “I love to go to the beach and fish.” Dad smiled from ear to ear. “I think I could do that every day, from nine to five, without an alarm clock to wake me up.”

Clifton nodded with a tight expression as he stared at his plate.

“Do you know what I do instead?” Another rhetorical question. “I go to work. Every day. Whether I *feel* like it or not.”

Mom set serving bowls on the table, and her and Dad dug in.

Clifton had lost his appetite.

“You get what I'm saying, son?” Dad said.

"Sure," he answered, rubbing the back of his neck, and staring intently at his empty plate.

"Good," Dad said. "Today just wasn't your day for archery, I get it, but you've committed to Mr. Anderson this year. He depends on you to help out with the younger kids who are new. You've been there longer than anyone else, and you're one of the best archers I know. It's just once a month. Don't let it happen again, okay?"

Clifton gave Dad a thumb's up gesture, his hunger miraculously returned. He scooped rice, chicken, and broccoli onto his plate and inhaled deeply. Mom was a great cook. Maybe not as good as Liv the dwarf. Everything she cooked was fresh and rich and mouthwatering. It could've been that they used less pesticides in the Middle Ages or because she, herself, tended to the animals and vegetables he had eaten. If he ever did get the courage to talk to his parents about time travel and mythical creatures, he'd be sure to leave Liv's cooking out. Wouldn't want to hurt Mom's feelings.

"Hope everyone's hungry," Mom said putting a plate on the tray of Pierce's highchair. He stared at the broccoli and his face scrunched in disgust. Clifton snickered.

"Looks delicious, honey," Dad said.

Clifton relaxed as Mom and Dad talked about their days, laughing as Pierce flung small bits of broccoli off his plate with tiny, plump fingers. Each time he did, Mom set a new piece on his tray, which made it even funnier. Clifton tried showing Pierce how delicious broccoli was by over-exaggerating each bite, but it only made Pierce smash his vegetable into his rice.

"So, Clifton," Dad started. "Mom said you didn't want to take the new archery set to club today, so I thought maybe you and I could go to Wickham Park tomorrow and give them a whirl. Just the two of us, with no one else watching."

"You've been begging your father and I for your own bow and arrows for years," Mom added, "and now that you have them, it's like you want to forget they exist."

If Mom only knew.

"Yeah, buddy. Do you not like them?"

Clifton felt rice wedge in his throat. He swallowed hard. What if the Arrows of Light took Clifton and his dad to 1485? "I don't know, Dad. I'm kind of tired of archery. Maybe I've outgrown it."

Mom and Dad exchanged a glance.

"Nonsense. You don't outgrow something like archery," Dad said. "It runs in your blood."

"It does?"

"Sure, it does. Your grandpa used to take me out in the woods to shoot turkeys and deer when I was a boy, and his father, your great grandpa, did the same with him. Actually, your great-great grandpa, Samuel, was a famous archer."

"Like Robin Hood," Mom added with a smile. "We should watch that tonight."

Dad grinned. "He was almost that good. But he did enter into archery contests with those same arrows you now have."

"Were they the same arrows you and grandpa used?"

"No. Grandpa Samuel's bow and arrows went missing for years. I remember as a kid being told they'd been taken away by some mysterious creature because they were magic, if you can believe that." Dad laughed.

Clifton nearly shot milk out his nose.

"I know," Dad responded. "Magic arrows...crazy, right?"

"Sure, Dad. Crazy."

"Then after your great grandpa moved into the retirement place, we found Grandpa Samuel's arrows in the attic. Searched a million times up there, and never found them."

"Right after you were born," Mom added.

"That's right," Dad said, eyes bright with excitement. "Your great-grandpa used to joke that the arrows chose you, that they'd arrived because you were born."

Clifton barely listened, the story of the arrow's arrival coinciding with his birth almost too much to bear.

"Yep. Part of the reason why we put him in the home was because your great-grandpa was starting to say things that didn't make a whole lot of sense." Dad stood, carrying his plate to the sink. "Anyway, give it some thought. About tomorrow, I mean. I know I've been busy with work lately and I really think we could use some guy time together."

"Okay, Dad. Sounds good."

Dad's forehead wrinkled as his eyes widened. "Great. We'll head out early and grab a bite after." He leaned over to kiss Mom on the cheek. "Great dinner, sweetheart. Need help cleaning up?"

"Clifton can help. You go get comfy and find us a film for movie night."

Clifton helped his mom clear the table as Dad went to change. Pierce had managed to mash all his broccoli in his rice and glob that all over the table. Mom cleaned it up, wiping down Pierce's face and hands, as he squirmed and squealed in his seat.

"Should've just eaten it," Clifton told him, as he loaded the dishwasher.

The dinner chores done, and Pierce nestled in his toddler bed, the rest of the Chase family sat in the living room to watch *Robin Hood.* Clifton loved Saturday movie night, even if he did fall asleep in the middle of the film.

It was late when Mom woke him on the couch and walked him to his bedroom. It was even later when a sound he couldn't place startled him enough to sit upright. He scanned his room, found nothing, and slowly laid back down. It must have been a dream. As he closed his eyes, a crash from his closet shot him into overdrive and the light that spilled out from beneath the door confirmed he wasn't dreaming. Clifton grabbed a baseball bat and tiptoed closer. His heart thudded in his chest as he turned the knob and flung the door wide opened in a single movement, bat raised, ready to strike the intruder. Only the three-foot tall creature standing before him stopped him dead in his tracks.

Chapter Five
Sleepwalking

"Do not hurt me," the creature begged.

Clifton lowered the bat, his eyes pinned on the pointy-eared, dark-eyed being that stood in his closet. It held a Medieval-styled lantern between fat fingers, with the long nose and jutting chin of a brownie, he guessed.

"What are you doing in my closet?"

"Oh, I beg forgiveness, sir. I wasn't aware of the boundaries of your land. I am a mere hobthrush, on a great mission, of which you were not supposed to be part."

"Well, I am part…now. That sort of happens when you break and enter."

"Oh, no, sir. Hobbie has not broken anything that belongs to Clifton Chase." He slapped an oversized hand over his mouth and Clifton noticed dirt embedded beneath his yellowed nails.

"You know my name. Who sent you?" Clifton reached for the hobthrush, who slipped to the back of his closet. The goblin screeched, a loud blaring foghorn that would wake up everyone. Clifton gripped the creature by the arm, twisted sideways, and planted a firm hand over its mouth, until sharp teeth tore into his knuckles. He yowled in pain and shook his hand free as he heard a rap on his door.

"Clifton?"

It was his mother. He yanked at a jacket hanging in his closet and wrapped up the creature in one swift flip before he sat down on top to silence him. He blew out the lantern as his bedroom door swung opened and his mom walked in.

"Hey, Mom," he said, as casually as possible. The creature squirmed and Clifton started impromptu bouncing to hold it in place.

"Clifton, what are you doing in your closet? It's the middle of the night."

"Just exercising," he replied, as if it were the most normal thing to do. "Trying out some workouts I saw online."

"Now?" Her eyebrows lifted high.

"Yeah, Mom. Everybody knows the witching hour is when you burn the most calories."

"There's a witching hour workout?"

"Mh-hm."

"Whose videos are you watching? You know what...Never mind. We can talk about this in the morning. I thought I heard you scream."

"Nope. It's all about the breathing, Mom." He tried hard to come across as an expert. "If you want to really feel the burn, you have to hold your breath until you can't hold it any longer, and then when you let it out it sounds like you're screaming, when you're not."

Arms crossed, head tilted, and eyes squinted, Mom clearly showed all the signs that she didn't believe a single word coming out of his mouth. This was not looking good for Clifton.

"I see what's going on here," she finally said.

He swallowed hard, still bouncing. "You...uh…you do?"

"Yup. You're getting older, Clifton, and your body is going through changes that--"

"God, no. Mom! I just sleepwalked, okay? I was having a dream that I was working out and woke up in my closet, and I screamed. There, I said it." Clifton sputtered words as quickly as possible so his mom couldn't start the 'birds and bees' speech. "Sleepwalking. That's it."

With a satisfied smile, like she'd found the Holy Grail, Mom said, "No more weird videos about night workouts, okay?"

"Great idea, Mom."

"And how about you get back to bed now?"

"Sure thing." Mom stared at him waiting. Clifton tilted his head. "Mom, I'm embarrassed enough. Do you have to watch me crawl back into my bed, too?"

"Oh!" Mom covered her eyes as a joke. "Of course, sweetie. Sometimes I forget how much you're growing, and you don't need me like you used to."

Clifton just nodded. "I love you, Mom."

"Love you too, sweetie. Good night."

"Night," he said, and then his bedroom door closed.

Clifton flipped off the hobthrush, his hand immediately covering the creature's wide mouth. “Now you listen here. If you promise not to make a sound, I'll take my hand off your mouth. Deal?”

The wide-eyed being nodded swiftly.

“Okay. I'm taking off my hand now.” Slowly, Clifton slid back his hand and the hobthrush breathed in quickly, apologizing repeatedly for his rudeness and *breaking-in-entering*.

“What's your name, creature?” Clifton asked.

“I am called Hobbie, sir.”

“And why are you here, Hobbie?”

“I am on my master's bidding. He implored I retrieve the arrows from Clifton Chase in the Closet of the Bed-Room.”

Clifton grabbed Hobbie hard. “Who sent you here? What is your master's name?”

“The Prince sent me,” Hobbie squealed. “Prince John of Nottingham.”

Chapter Six
Journey

Clifton knew the name well, and he didn't doubt he misheard the hobthrush when it mentioned it. Instead, he welcomed this lucid launch into a very vivid dream as the result of too much chemically buttered popcorn and unsanctioned *Robin Hood* in the same night. He willed it away, squinted hard, and demanded he wake up. When he opened his eyes, he met a fraught faced hobthrush, staring like Clifton was the crazy in the room.

"Please, sir. You must let me go. Or the sheriff will beat Hobbie."

"And that's the sheriff..."

"Of Nottingham, sir."

"Right," Clifton said. "I don't think so."

"Oh, but he will. The Sheriff beats Hobbie for every wrongdoing, even if I know not the nature of the wrong done."

"That's not what I meant." Clifton stared at the small, petrified creature. "Do you have proof?"

"Proof? Well, sir, if you allow me to move, I can show you on my back--"

"Not of the beatings, that you're really from Nottingham."

But Hobbie had already twisted his wrist and loosened his hand, which reached for the Arrow of Light.

"Not so fast," Clifton said, grabbing his arm. "I don't have a problem with you leaving, but you're not taking my arrows with you."

The hobthrush's eyes shimmered, filled with tears, and he wailed so loudly that Clifton was forced to cover Hobbie's mouth and push him down to the floor again.

"You have got to stay quiet," Clifton whispered harshly. "Or we'll both get in big trouble."

The hobthrush nodded and his body stopped convulsing.

When Hobbie was seated upright again, and his tears mere sniffles, Clifton asked, "Why does your master need the arrows? Does he have a match with Robin Hood or something?" Clifton snorted at his own joke.

Hobbie's eyes widened and he whispered, "You know Robin of Loxley?"

"Who doesn't? He's only the best archer in history. Ever. I mean, the guy's a legend. They've written books about him and filmed movies about him, well, about who they think he was, anyway. A lot of it's made up, like Santa Claus. They were both based on real people, but how much of it can anyone truly know?"

Hobbie stared and for the first time since Clifton met him, he was quiet. "What?" Clifton asked.

"I was not expecting someone like you to possess the arrows. You are a boy, small and weak. I thought the arrows chose only the strongest, bravest of men. Not, the likes...of you."

"Jeez. No filter there. I'm beginning to understand why the Sheriff beats you, Hobbie."

Hobbie's mouth twitched on one side. "Well, it was my pleasure to meet you, sir, but my allotted time has expired, and I must leave now."

"Not with my grandpa's arrows, you're not."

"Grand Pause? Hobbie is not familiar."

"It doesn't matter. The Arrows of Light stay and you go."

Hobbie's lip trembled again and his eyes watered, but before he could break into a wailing sob, Clifton threw him against the back wall of his closet and said, "If you tell me why the Sheriff needs my arrows, I might change my mind." He had no intention of following through, of course, but hoped to squeeze some info out of the timid being.

"Oh, many thanks, Clifton Chase. Many thanks. Your kindness will be told in stories and legends to come, for--"

"Right now, Hobbie, or I'll make you leave empty-handed."

Hobbie covered his own mouth this time, and Clifton tried not to laugh. He slowly lowered his hand and said in a whisper, "If Hobbie returns without the

Arrows of Light, Hobbie will be beaten to death, sir. So, you see, I must take them."

"Why does the Sheriff need them?"

"Not the Sheriff, Prince John. For an archery competition, sir, between my lord and your Robin Hood. While the Prince is an excellent marksman, he believes the Arrows of Light will improve his chances to win in the tournament."

"Basically, he needs to cheat to win."

"Winning is everything to the Prince, sir. He has gone through great lengths before to ensure as much. Now you see why I must take your Grand Pause arrows."

Clifton puffed his cheeks, then blew out the air. On the one hand, Robin Hood wasn't real, and this was simply a very vivid lucid dream, making this conversation questionable. On the other hand, he was holding a hobthrush and Clifton had met dwarves, giants, dragons, and mermaids, meaning he might not be dreaming. He needed to know for sure.

"Tell me, Hobbie, about this tournament. It must be pretty important for the Prince to have sent you all the way here to steal my arrows."

"Oh, Hobbie only planned to borrow Clifton Chase's arrows, sir. And yes. It is of the upmost importance to the Prince."

Clifton didn't want to ask, but he had to. "What happens if he wins?"

"The imprisonment of Robin Hood. He will serve out his remaining days in the dungeon on Castle Rock in Nottingham."

"But if Robin Hood is captured, who will fight for the poor? Who will be their voice?"

“Those are concerns for politicians and not servants such as Hobbie.”

Clifton couldn't let this happen. If Prince John used an Arrow of Light against anyone, even Robin Hood, he would surely win. Fact or fiction, any world where Robin Hood lost, and Nottingham won was a very bad one. But those weren't Clifton's problems. It wasn't his job to rewrite history, but he could at least make it harder for the Prince, couldn’t he?

“I tell you what, Hobbie,” Clifton said, holding out the lantern. “Why don't you take this and go back from wherever you came from. My arrows are staying here with me.”

Hobbie took the lantern. “Very well, Clifton Chase. If it must be this way, there is not much Hobbie can do.”

“Well, I'm glad we finally found a--”

But Hobbie snapped his fingers, igniting the lantern. The brilliance of the intense flame forced Clifton to shield his eyes. In that moment, Hobbie shifted out of his grip, a blur between coats and clothes, until the room once again fell dark. Clifton gave his eyes a moment to readjust from temporary blindness, and when he could see again, his heart sank.

Both Hobbie and the Arrows of Light were gone.

Chapter Seven
Familiar

De Laura Middle School stood a block from the Atlantic Ocean. With outside hallways and two stories, a view of the waves breaking on a good, clear day was probable. Clifton didn't surf and hated sand scratching his skin. He preferred chess and archery, skills that required study and thoughtful deliberation, neither of which made him the most popular kid in school.

A week had passed since archery club, since meeting Hobbie, and losing the Arrows of Light. Forced to lie through his teeth, he'd told Dad his elbow joint pulled in his sleep from night exercising too hard after sleepwalking, something so ridiculous, Dad had no desire to argue.

Between second and third periods, Clifton turned the corner of the upstairs open hall, where Ryan Rivales towered over two kids Clifton had never seen before. A gathered crowd witnessed the spectacle, forming a shield from any teachers prowling the halls.

"Why'd you get in my way?" Ryan asked the first kid.

"I'm s-s-sorry," he stuttered. "I didn't s-s-see you."

Ryan mimicked, "You're s-s-sorry? Didn't s-s-see me? Give me a break, Stutter."

"Don't make fun of my brother," the second kid said.

Ryan's attention shifted to Stutter's brother, who cowered back. The promise of action diminishing, the crowd lost interest and several students raced the bell realizing no fight was happening today. In a ditch effort to save face, Ryan stepped forward, grabbed Stutter's brother by his shirt, and lifted the scrawny kid into the air. The rubberneckers bounded back, and Ryan smirked. Clifton watched from the sidelines. The boys reminded him of Prince Edward and Richard from 1485 England. The resemblance was striking with the older brother having dark hair and the younger fair skinned.

"Please," the fair-skinned brother begged Ryan. "I don't want trouble. Just leave us alone."

Ryan's hand pulled back into a fist and, as he prepared to punch, Clifton grabbed hold, whipped him around, and shoved him into the wall. The boy Ryan released was steadied by his brother and the two blended in with the surrounding students.

Ryan launched off the bricks and slammed into Clifton. "What's your problem, Chase?"

"I don't have a problem."

"You do now. You're always sticking your nose in where it don't belong."

Clifton turned his back on Ryan. "Whatever, dude."

"Don't walk away from me," Ryan said, shoving Clifton so hard he fell on the concrete floor. He pushed quickly to his feet and faced his foe. "You want more?" Ryan asked.

"I just want you to leave people alone, man. Or try picking on the wrestling team captain for a change, not the smallest kids in the school." Clifton faced the new kids. "No offense, dudes."

The brothers nodded. They probably weighed a buck-fifty together, soaking wet.

"What are you gonna do to stop me?" Ryan asked.

"I'm not gonna do anything. Just...grow up. What's the matter with you?"

He turned to walk away again, when Ryan threw a pen at the back of his head. It stung for a second, but Clifton ignored him and kept walking. The fire burned out in Ryan's fight and the crowd dissipated as the bell rang. Ryan waved everyone off as swarming bugs and his posse headed to class.

The brothers glided over to Clifton. "Thank you," the fair-skinned one said.

"You guys okay?" he asked.

"Yes, thanks to you," the dark-haired boy added. "I'm Ed, and this is my brother Richie."

Under his breath, Clifton said, "You've got to be kidding me."

"We owe you," Richie added.

Clifton smirked. “Random question, but do your parents like history?”

The boys' faces lit up. “Yes. We were named after--”

“King Richard's nephews, I know,” Clifton interrupted. “My name's Clifton.”

“Cool,” Ed said. “You like history too?”

With his hands fanning out to the sides, Clifton said, “For me, history feels alive.”

The boys laughed, and Clifton joined them nervously.

The second bell rang.

“Well, we're late,” Ed said to Richie. Facing Clifton, he added, “Thank you, Clifton, for helping us. See you around.”

“Any time,” Clifton said, as the boys trotted off. “Apparently any time in the past, present, *or* future.”

Chapter Eight
Alone

Clifton mobilized on the battlefield; a notched arrow aimed upon his enemy. As if in a film, with the sound stretched and the speed slowed, a brutal king released an arrow into his nephew, Richard, knocking the boy to the grassy knoll. Edward, the older of the two princes, sprinted the field, his wide mouth muted by the soundtrack playing in Clifton's mind.

Then, the dream twisted into a nightmare, and King Richard III trained his arrow upon Clifton. His face turned in a sneer, dark eyes focused, the bully king released, and Clifton knew what happened next. No matter how many times he dreamed this dream, Dane the dwarf always lunged as a buffer and caught the arrow in his chest. Clifton woke up as Dane died in his arms, the endpoint of this recurring nightmare.

Like he had in 1485, during the real Battle of Bosworth Field.

Death's hand was precise and unrelenting even with the holy grail in Clifton's grasp. Why hadn't Dane let him use the healing magic in the fletching to save him? The feathers from the mythical beast, Simurgh, could easily have overpowered Death's grip, releasing the dwarf.

Lying in the dark, Clifton stared at his ceiling. A tear trailed down his cheek and soaked into his pillowcase. He rolled over, tried to fall back asleep, but knew he wouldn't for some time. Deliberating never worked as he struggled to persuade his heart that he'd made the right decision in letting Dane die.

He regretted it above all else.

He couldn't forgive himself.

He imagined the dream was triggered by meeting those two boys at school, the ones who so closely resembled his friends from the past. Where did they come from, anyway? Was it simply a strange coincidence? Clifton knew better.

The sun brushed the horizon painting the morning sky in soft shades of orange sherbet. Even though it was crazy early, Clifton got dressed. He needed a change of setting or else he'd go mad replaying the hobthrush's thievery of the Arrows of Light. He'd a strange sensation he should go to Wickham Park.

Pierce sat on the living room floor watching cartoons while Mom fixed breakfast. "Aren't you up early," Mom said, frying bacon.

"I'm gonna head up to the archery field for a little while. Is that all right?"

"Sure. I guess. Is everything okay? It's pretty early for you to be up and out on a Saturday."

Clifton grabbed a piece of bacon from the pile Mom set cooling on the metal rack. “I had a bad dream. I don't think I can fall back asleep, so I thought I'd get some practice in before the field fills up.”

“You want to talk about it?”

“Nah,” Clifton said, shaking his head. “It was just a dream.”

Mom grinned. “Don't be too long, okay? Just an hour. And don't talk to any strangers no matter how nice they seem. Keep your phone on and text regularly.”

“Okay, Mom. I know. This isn't my first time going to the park alone.”

“I go, too?” Pierce called from the living room.

Clifton walked over and picked up his little brother. “Not today, Pierce. I'm going all by myself.”

“Like a big boy?”

“Yup. Like a big boy.”

“I go by myself with you, like a big boy?”

Mom and Clifton laughed.

“Maybe when you're older,” Clifton said. “I can bring you back some cool leaves. Would you like that? Would you like me to bring back some leaves?”

Pierce clapped his hands. “Yes! Yes! Leaves.”

Clifton set his brother down, grabbed a water bottle, a snack, and some sunblock that Mom insisted he tote along. He put it all into his backpack and headed out the door.

“Clifton,” Mom called, “just an hour, okay?”

“Okay, Mom,” he answered back.

But for some reason, he didn't think he was telling her the truth.

Chapter Nine
Pearl

Clifton's neighborhood sat within walking distance of Wickham Park. Near the back edge of the property, campsites and RV lots, filled nearly year-round, brought back memories of Boy Scout weekends with tug-of-war matches over mud pools, s'mores roasting in fire pits, and nighttime exploring with his friends.

Clifton turned down the dirt road near the sign that stated: ARCHERY FIELD - ARCHERS ONLY. The path curved to an open lot, then bent a second time to a straightaway intersecting several rows of archery lanes. Each lane ended with a bull's eye painted on a wooden target. Clifton did a double-take at a shadow moving among the hedges. He wondered if it were Hobbie, the crafty creature who'd managed to steal the Arrows of Light right out from beneath Clifton's nose. Should he have done more to protect them? They were, after all, headed for the hands of another tyrant.

But who was he kidding?

Prince John and the Sheriff of Nottingham weren't real people. Were they? Maid Marion and Robin Hood were book characters loosely based on the real lives of historic figures, more like metaphors than literal descriptions. He probably should've looked that up online before he left his house. But the dream with Dane and the princes had been so vivid, he wasn't thinking straight. He'd had enough good sense to bring along his compound bow, so Mom wouldn't ask questions, even if he didn't plan on using it.

Clifton pumped his legs and the early morning air washed over his skin. He wished it were a normal day and he were a normal kid. But those days were long gone. He'd been chosen by the Arrows of Light.

Even if he no longer possessed them.

The straightaway ended at the archery field opening to equally spaced targets framing the far edge. Clifton had spent years in this part of the park shooting to improve his skills. He remembered the first time he shot the Arrow of Light, before he knew it was magic, how it drew him deep across The Hinterland, into the woods, and through time.

Would he still shoot the arrow today, knowing what power it held and the havoc it would wreak?

Probably...

Clifton leaned his bike against a tree and set down his archery equipment. His heart grew heavy as he stared at the barren field, thinking of his friends from the past: the princes, Dane the dwarf and his wife, Liv, and the beautiful creature named Simurgh.

He'd let them all down, and he'd never have the chance to make things right.

As he crossed the field, hands in his pockets, he felt led to keep going. He passed the practice zone that preceded The Hinterland, ducked among the trees, and followed the path to the embankment. He skirted the shed where Mr. Anderson kept the equipment, until he reached the large lake that spread out through the center of the park, surrounded by a paved sidewalk and lush woodlands. Boughs of oaks, frozen in an eternal grasp for limbs on the opposite shore, shaded the water that rippled with small insects and dragonflies.

Clifton sat.

He plucked grass.

He watched it float.

A tightness gripped his chest. Why had he felt led to the lake? There was nothing in it to help him. Even if he wanted to do something, which he didn't, he had no direction to find the arrows or use their magic. He couldn't time travel or conjure Simurgh or use his mind to transport himself to wherever the Arrows of Light had landed.

"If I'm supposed to go, then it'll happen," he said out loud.

As if on cue, the lake began to bubble and rumble like boiling water in a pot and Clifton jumped to his feet. Through the surface, a round object poked up and then launched into the air before plunging back in.

It couldn't be Clifton thought. *Could it?*

The surface back to glass, he inched closer until his face hovered above his reflection in the lake, which he stared through waiting to see her clearly. Pearl, the

Siren from Cantre'r Gwaelod surfaced and waded in the water, smiling widely.

Chapter Ten
Second Chance

"Hello, again, Clifton Chase," Pearl said in her sing-song way. Her voice conjured a mix of Christmas morning, scoring the final goal in the game, and fresh baked chocolate-chip cookies pulled hot from the oven. She was, after all, a Siren.

"I can't believe you're...how are you? I just…wow!"

She giggled. "It is wonderful to see you, too, my friend."

Clifton shook his head and crouched beside her. "I never thought I'd see you again. I mean, when you were helping me escape Cantre'r Gwaelod and I watched Excalibur zip past toward you, I didn't know if it would reach you in time."

She placed her arms on the river's edge and laid her heart-shaped chin on top. "Didn't Simurgh deliver my message?"

"Well, sure," Clifton said. "She said you escaped. But King Gwyddno was pretty mad you let me go, so I was...you know...a little worried about you."

Pearl smiled. "I see. You were kind to worry."

Clifton's face grew warm as he sat on the bank, plucking grass. He wanted to be closer to her, to wade in the water too. She had that effect on people, especially boys. Then, like storm clouds rolling in to block the sun, everything grew suddenly cold and dark and ominous. "You're here about the arrows, aren't you? You heard they went missing and someone's sent for me, haven't they?"

"Yes," she answered. "Your attendance is required."

"I'm not in any trouble, am I? There isn't, like, some mystical court I have to appear before and face sentencing, right?"

"Not at all." Pearl laughed and slipped underwater, leaving Clifton staring at the bubbles she'd left behind.

His head instantly cleared of her presence. "Why did she laugh at me? I didn't say anything funny. I was being serious."

She surfaced, and her magic, like a lingering scent, reached his brain, where her small smile eased his negative thoughts. "No one is after you, Clifton Chase. "Not yet anyway."

He stared into her shiny eyes. "What do you mean, 'not yet'?"

"We need your help."

Jumping up, Clifton said, "Forget it. Not again. Do you have any idea how hard I've worked to delete all that stuff from my memory about the princes and their uncle and, well, all of it?" He couldn't say out loud what he was really trying to forget. Dane died saving Clifton's life and he could've saved his instead.

"Why would you ever want to forget?" Pearl splashed her mermaid tail.

He was a boy living in the twenty-first century, where magic and mythology were make-believe. Where Sirens didn't exist. Where King Richard III and his nephew princes lived on the pages of history books and nowhere else. Shrugging, Clifton said, "I just do, all right?"

"Well, I don't believe you for one second. The boy I met was brave and kind, someone who cared about his friends and would do anything to help them."

"And one of those friends died."

Pearl touched his arm. "If you had saved Dane, the princes would've died and their brother-in-law, Henry, would never have taken his place on the throne as King. You would have altered history into a timeline too dangerous to be allowed to exist. Dane knew all of this. He did what he did on purpose, with purpose."

Clifton's jaw tightened. "It still doesn't make it fair."

"True, but sometimes the scale is not weighted the same on both sides, and our only answer is to do what's right, knowing others would do the same for us if we needed them to. Your friends will help you, Clifton."

Clifton looked up at her. "What friends?"

"Prince John has possession of the Arrows of Light. His wizards are using dark magic to try and forge them into one massive arrow. He has already challenged Robin of Loxley to an archery competition in five days, at which time he plans to unveil this weapon. If Robin loses, Prince John will have the Sheriff of Nottingham arrest him and he will be hanged. If this happens, Clifton, there will be no one left to be the voice for the poor of Sherwood Forest or the commoners of Nottingham."

Clifton paced as he spoke. "Robin Hood is the greatest archer of all time. He won't have any problem in a competition involving bows, arrows, and targets. Believe me."

"You do not understand, Clifton. The Arrow of Light you used to defeat King Richard III was one of five forged by Time in the beginning. Imagine its power magnified, tripled. There is no archer, no matter how skilled, who can compete against it and win. Robin Hood does not stand a chance if that weapon is forged. You must help. The people of Nottingham need you."

Clifton stopped pacing. "A second ago, you said my friends would help me. I don't have friends in Sherwood Forest, especially not during the time of Robin Hood."

"Not entirely the way you think. Sherwood Forest neighbors Griffon Forest, where Dane lives. He will help you; he just doesn't know you need it yet."

"Woah, woah...wait a minute. Dane is dead."

"The Dane you knew died in 1485 England. But in 1199, the time we will be entering, Dane Englewood is a boy, the son of Drathco, King of the dwarves and one of the most powerful dwarves in Griffon Forest.

Dwarves, you see, have much longer life spans than humans."

A shiver played the discs down Clifton's spine. Was he being given a second chance? "If Dane is still alive and you can take me to him, I'll do it. How do we get there?"

"I thought you'd never ask," Pearl said. She handed him a gelatinous mask; the kind he'd used before to breathe underwater.

"Well, here we go again," Clifton said, and he dove into the cool lake.

Chapter Eleven
Dwarfed

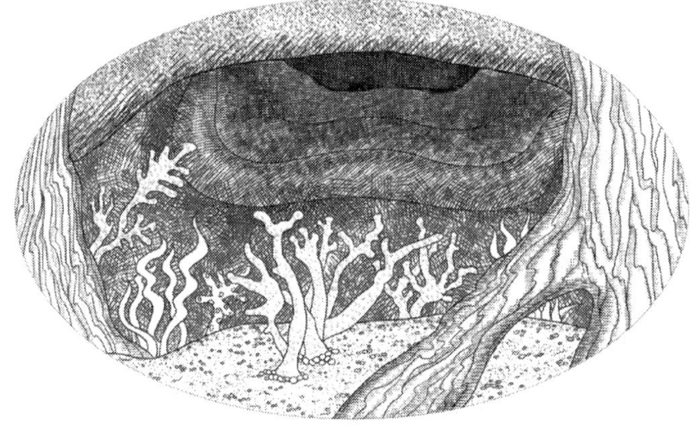

Clifton hesitated to breathe. From experience, he knew the snug fitting organic creature on his face was called a *fir mask*, an organism that converted his carbon dioxide into oxygen for symbiotic survival. He'd swam the depths of the English Channel wearing one once, to an ancient underwater city, and had been perfectly capable of breathing normally. His mind grasped this truth and simultaneously rejected it. Instinct glued his mouth closed until the fir mask squirmed so much it forced him to surrender his captive breath.

He took in his surroundings. He'd never seen the lake from this angle before. It was quite lovely. Once they pressed through the murky tannin, to a fathomless depth beyond what the lake's dimensions allowed, his clarity grew crystal clear. Reeds waved in the currents. Small schools of fish swam past. Billions of tiny bubbles billowed out of bushes, shimmering diamonds in a pool of glass. A largemouth bass crossed in front of him and the fir mask became a brake, flipping him head over heels and toppling into the startled fish. When Clifton righted himself, the lake was empty, and Pearl was nowhere to be seen.

Slowly, panic ebbed up from his chest as he moved through the murky water, his vision cut to barely beyond an arm's length ahead. Where had all the fish gone? Or the reeds and bushes of the lake? More importantly where was Pearl? It was like a bad dream he'd had since he was little, one in which he stared up at the surface of a lake from its bottom, unable to move or swim, knowing he'd drown if he didn't try. But which way was up? He never should have jumped into the stupid lake.

He began to swim toward what he hoped was the surface, when he felt Pearl's hand take his own. She led them to a deep ridge that curved back and opened up into an underwater cavern. Clifton couldn't believe this amazing rock formation lay below the surface of a lake in Wickham Park. He wondered if maybe they had already time-travelled or world jumped, the sight too incredible to believe.

Waving him on, Pearl disappeared into the cave entrance that suddenly resembled a monstrous catfish mouth. Clifton gulped and swam lower into the cloudy water, passing reeds that had become trees whose trunks went out of sight below him, much, much deeper, he knew, then the lakebed. He entered the dark cave, peering over his shoulder at the open water one last time, before he was blinded by coal blackness on every side.

"Pearl," he said on instinct. This caused the fir mask to squirm on his face in discomfort. Apparently, this organism didn't like it when Clifton spoke.

Using his arms for eyes, he felt around until he reached the back of the cave. He shuffled his hands across the wall, for what he thought was long enough to find something, anything, but the wall kept spreading, kept curving. He couldn't even find the entrance anymore. Clifton shuddered. The water had turned very, very cold.

Suddenly, the ground fell from beneath him, as the water flushed out, like he was in a giant's toilet bowl. He grappled with the wall for a knob or an overlay to grip onto, but the algae-coating was too slick. He was going to get sucked into the vortex, and worse, the fir mask leapt off his face, abandoning ship, leaving Clifton unable to breathe. Feet first, the water yanked him through, pulled him in different directions, and forced him to follow its path, until the swirling slowed, and the pressure ceased.

But he still couldn't breathe.

A pinprick of light hovered above him, like in his dream, and he swam toward it, through water much clearer than the lake in Wickham Park. With his lungs burning, his legs pumped as hard as they could, knowing his instinct would open his mouth any second to take a last watery breath. And right before his lungs released, Pearl swam in front of him.

And she kissed him.

It was like he'd seen the lagoon mermaids do with Peter Pan, kissing in a breath to keep him alive. It was just enough to get him to the surface, where he struggled onto the shore and coughed up the water he'd inhaled. Pearl swam nearby, watching closely, until Clifton was able to sit upright.

"Are you better?" she asked.

He side-smiled. "I am thanks to you."

"It was the least I could do, seeing the fir mask jumped off your face at the most inopportune time."

"Tell me about it." Looking around, Clifton confirmed they were no longer in Wickham Park. The trees were different. The air wasn't so stale. The sky looked younger. "Where are we?" he said. "I mean, when are we...no... first, where are we?"

With a giggle that warmed his cheeks she said, "We are back in Griffon Forest, though the time has changed. It's eleven-sixty-six in the spring." She pointed. "In that direction is a small cottage belonging to Drathco Englewood, his wife, and their son."

"Dane?"

She nodded quickly.

"Man, this is weird." Clifton stood. "Are you staying?"

She fanned out her arms. "I can't very well walk on land with a fish tail, now can I?" She did a flip in the water and waved her tail.

Clifton laughed. "I guess not. Will you be here to take me back?"

"We will meet again, my friend. Of that I am sure."

And as Pearl disappeared beneath the surface, Clifton stepped away from the lake, into the woods, toward the trail of smoke piping in the air that had to be coming from the dwarves' cottage.

Chapter Twelve
Reunion

Clifton plunged through curtains of pine, snapping twigs and crunching leaves along his path. As he neared the cottage, the front door flew open. High-spirited voices blew out like a gale, carrying a dwarf with fiery red hair, a bulbous nose, and the start of a beard. He stomped in Clifton's direction, forcing him to duck and cover behind some bushes. Was this Dane, his old friend? He seemed so young, though Clifton had no idea how dwarves looked in the various stages of their life span.

In the doorway, a much older dwarf—how he knew that, he couldn't say—with jet black hair along his head and a beard that stretched to the floor yelled, "If'n ya don't want my blood boilin' than jus' do what'n ya know yas suppose ta do, boy!"

"Yes, Pater," the young dwarf said, though Clifton saw him muttering to himself, "I don't need babysittin' like I'm some blasted fool."

Yup. That was Dane, all right.

He crossed the front yard path unsteady as a puppy on paws not yet grown into. Clifton kept pace using the trees as cover to sidle beside him in silence. It was hard to believe the young dwarf who appeared near his age was Dane.

"Who does he think he is anyway?" Dane asked no one. "Tellin' me who I can and cannot spend me time with?" He puffed out his chest and mockingly added, "I am Drathco Englewood, King of the Dwarves, and the biggest pain in the arse Griffon Forest has ever had the displeasure of housing."

Clifton covered his mouth to stifle a laugh. Dane was young and fiery. Nothing like the four-hundred-year-old he'd met in 1485, who was wise, stern, and mature. This dwarf stalked through the woods like a, well, like a child.

Stepping out of the foliage, Clifton tiptoed behind Dane, trying to decide his best approach. The first time they'd met, the little man already knew about Clifton. He was the one surprised. Now, roles were reversed, with Clifton knowing Dane and the one doing the surprising. But it was different. Clifton had read about dwarves in fairy tales. Though he doubted their existence, he at least recognized one when he saw one. The odds of a dwarf in the eleventh century having read tales of a boy in a t-shirt and sneakers roaming the woods was nil to none.

If only he had the Arrows of Light, then Dane would trust him.

If only he had the Arrows of Light, then he wouldn't be there.

As he followed at a safe distance, Clifton hoped Dane hadn't learned combat skills yet and better still, that the dwarf didn't carry any weapons. Crossing clumps of grass, occasional felled trees, and pebbles, Clifton decided he would introduce himself in the same manner that Dane had, by jumping on his back and pushing him to the ground. In the past, it had forced Clifton to listen so Dane could explain himself and gain his trust. It had worked then, and Clifton believed it would work now.

Dane trekked the trail, his mind maybe distracted by the fight he'd had with his dad, and seizing opportunity, Clifton closed in from the rear, matching step for step. Right, left. Right, left. Then, with a spring to his step, he launched through the air and landed on Dane's back. He pushed the little man to the ground, but in a nanosecond, the dwarf flipped him up, over, and down, knocking the breath out of him. Once again, Clifton's cheek scratched the earth as Dane sat on his back, holding his head down.

"I'm giving ya to three to tell me who ya are and why yer following me," Dane said.

Clifton had seen that go down much differently in his mind. He had no breath with which to reply, so the dwarf began the countdown.

"One."

Clifton still couldn't speak, his lungs emptied of oxygen.

"Two."

He forced his mouth to try and form words, as he heard the dwarf take a weapon out of his boot strap.

"Three."

As Dane's arm lifted to strike, Clifton finally had the air to yell, "Dane! Wait!"

The dwarf stopped mid-stride, then bent close to Clifton's ear and whispered, "How do ya know me name, boy? And dontcha be lyin' to me."

"Now that's a long story," Clifton said.

"Well, ya best get to talking then, because until ya start making sense, I'm not letting ya up."

Chapter Thirteen
Danger

It's funny how history tends to repeat itself. That's what Clifton was thinking as he sat pinned by the dwarf, tasting dirt, exactly like the first time they'd met. Well, history was about to change. "My name is Clifton Chase and I'm from the future."

Dane pressed harder into Clifton's back. "I told ya, dontcha be lying' to me, boy."

Clifton flinched. "I'm not! How else do you think I know who you are, Dane Englewood, son of Drathco, King of the Dwarves?" Nothing. "Ever seen garments like these before?" Clifton kicked his sneaker into Dane's back. He didn't move or say a word. "Fine. I'm a sorcerer disguised as boy here to capture you and feed you to a dragon. Come on, man. Aren't you even the slightest bit curious?"

After a few seconds of silent debate, Dane sighed and scooted off. Clifton stood, brushing himself clean of matted leaves. He looked Dane over, his forehead wrinkled in curiosity, and Clifton couldn't help himself. He began to laugh.

The dwarf closed the distance between them, his axe blade angled at Clifton's neck. "What's so funny?" he asked.

"Nothing, it's just...you're so young. I mean, how old are you anyway?"

"Forty-three and a half."

"Really?"

"That's fourteen in human years. Dwarves live to be hundreds of years, unlike humans." Dane shook his head. "But yer changing the subject. Tell me how ya know me name."

Clifton rubbed the back of his neck and squinted. "We've met before, man. But I can't explain it because you won't believe me."

"If ya don't start making sense soon, boy, I'm gonna put yer face back in the dirt."

Clifton's arms blocked his face instinctively. "Okay, okay. You showed up in my bedroom in, like, the twenty-first century, when you lived in the fifteenth century. It hasn't happened yet, for you, I mean."

"Why in blazes would I do that?"

"You needed the Arrow of Light that had--"

Dane clenched Clifton by the shirt. "How do ya know of such an arrow?"

"I told you. We've met." Images of Dane, future Dane, dying in Clifton's arms made his heart ache. "You brought me back to your time, to 1485, by way of Simurgh. Do you know her?"

"Of course, I know her. The question begs how do *you* know her?"

"Through you. She helped me when I needed it most."

Dane smiled his crooked little grin. "Aye. Sounds like Simurgh."

"And when I visited your cottage, you lived here with your wife, Liv."

"Olivia Lovegrove?" His face reddened to match his hair. "I would rather walk through the lair of a dragon, with a head cold, in me nightdress, than to ever imagine marrying that snobby, self-righteous dwarf."

"Wait, you wear a dress to bed?"

The dwarf glared.

Clifton smiled. "Well, I'm not sure what changed in that department, but you do marry her. And you do help me face a king, get back the Arrow of Light, and rescue two princes. Why else would I be here or say any of this if it weren't all true?"

The dwarf nodded, paced, and when he stopped, he faced Clifton and said, "I see yer point, Clifton was it? Now, what brings ya to Griffon Forest today?"

"The Arrow of Light again, only this time, there's three arrows gone missing."

"Well, I'm afraid yer mistaken. I have no such arrows in me possession. G'day." Dane advanced along the path on his father's business.

"I know," Clifton said, and Dane stopped short, causing Clifton to rush into his backside. "Sorry."

Dane grunted as he turned. "If ya know I don't carry the arrows, why are ya here buggin' me about 'em?"

"Because I need your help, Dane. You're the only one who can help me get the arrows back."

Dane stepped closer, his face inches from Clifton's. "You know who holds the Arrows of Light, dontcha?"

Clifton nodded. "Prince John and the Sheriff of Nottingham."

Dane stared off in the distance, taking several long moments to contemplate his position. "Well, guess now's as good a time as any to see if ya sink or swim."

"Swim. It's how I got here, actually. Do you know Pearl?"

"Who?"

"Never mind. Does this mean you'll help?"

The look in Dane's eyes was familiar, making Clifton's skin break into gooseflesh. "Aye, lad. If what yer saying is true, we are all in danger. Including yer future."

Chapter Fourteen
Memories

Clifton hid beside the dwarves' cottage until well after dusk. He shivered as the sun pulled its warmth from the world ushering in a cold, dark night. Dinnertime smells wafted through the opened windows and his stomach growled from salted potatoes, roasted meat, and fresh baked bread. Dane had told him to stay put until he could sneak Clifton inside, explaining how his father would never allow a human into his cottage.

He listened to the buzz of conversation and missed home. Missed his family. Even though he knew better, in quiet moments such as these, Clifton wondered if he were dreaming, caught up in a narrative of his own design. Then the scent of cherry vanilla laced tobacco hit him, and he recalled how Dane had smoked a pipe after dinner in 1485, a habit he imagined Drathco had passed down. He also remembered that after supper Liv had scooted around the side of the house to wash the dishes, and no sooner had he thought it, the front door swung open, painting a block of light on black earth.

Clifton hurried to the back of the house as Dane's mother turned the corner, following in his footsteps. He rushed all the way around to the far side of the cottage as Dane's mother reached the backyard, where she set the mound of plates and cups into the bin beside the water pump. She was a stout woman and Dane had her same wavy red hair, though hers was much longer. She hummed off-key as she washed, and Clifton tiptoed along the perimeter to where the scent of tobacco grew even stronger.

Clifton lifted to peer into the window of the den. A fire crackled and both Dane and his father faced the flames smoking their pipes on matching stools. Drathco had his eyes closed. Clifton waved his arms frantically to catch Dane's attention. The dwarf looked at him with a peaceful grin, looked away, then snapped his head back, shocked, as if he'd forgotten the boy stood outside his home, which he clearly had.

Dane jumped to his feet, startling his father awake, who yelled in a gruff voice, "What's the meaning of this, boy?"

Dane stuttered as he said, "The, uh..., chickens were...making noise. Maybe it's a wolf."

Drathco turned to the window, and Clifton ducked. "I hear nothing," Drathco said annoyed.

Clifton began making chicken clucks, very, very bad chicken clucks.

"Aye, it sounds like the chickens bein' torn apart right now. Listen to them sufferin'." Drathco stood to go check.

"I'll check it, Pater. Ya go couch a hogshead and let me see what's got them chickens in a tizzy."

Drathco nodded, extinguished his pipe, and stood with a yawn. "That's a good lad. Best get yerself to sleep soon after."

"Aye, Pater. Till morrow."

"Till morrow, boy," Drathco harrumphed, his footfalls heavy on the wood floor.

Clifton slowly rose to peer through the window. Dane waved him toward the back of the cottage and Clifton mimed that his mother was doing the dishes there, so Dane pointed toward the front of the cottage and Clifton nodded.

The front door creaked opened and Clifton stepped into the warm foyer. Behind him, the door closed with a soft click and the two crept quietly down the hall until passing the kitchen, at which point Clifton's stomach growled loud enough to garner a stern glare from Dane. Clifton shrugged his apologies and they continued through the den, where Drathco's snores carried from his bedroom so loudly, they should have woken him up.

As they neared the hall, which Clifton remembered led to the bedrooms, the front door opened with a bang and Dane's mother trucked inside with clean dishes. Drathco swore, his heavy stomps crossed the floor, and he peered out to see what all the ruckus was. Clifton's eyes nearly popped out of his head in fear, and Dane shoved him between the two chairs he and his father had sat on moments earlier.

Dane stood in such a way that he blocked Drathco's view of the boy. His mother, well, Clifton hoped she wouldn't look.

"Blasted, women. Ya trying to wake the dead?"

"Drathco, love. Couching the hogshead already? My, my. Ya should be getting out more in the daytime. Fresh air'll do ya some good."

He harrumphed again and slammed the door behind him. Dane shuffled around the chairs, so he was now blocking Clifton from his mother's view. He kicked him, and tipped his head toward the hall, to which Clifton got the message.

As he moved to stand, Dane's mother said, "Whatchya think yer doing?"

Clifton froze, crouched between the two chairs behind Dane's frame. He thought for sure they'd been busted.

"Hang these pots for your dear mater, would ya?"

"Sure thing," Dane answered. As he stepped forward to grab the pots, he kicked Clifton again, and the boy shot like a bullet into the shadows of the hall, only feeling safe when the sound of Drathco's snores filled his ears.

After Dane helped with the pots and pan, he walked to where Clifton waited in the hallway. "Well, good night," he said, forcing a yawn.

"Going to bed so soon, are ya, my love?"

Clifton crouched behind the dwarf beneath the dark covering of his shadow, holding his breath.

"Sure am tired, Mater. That meal was so delicious it brought on sleep. See, listen to Pater."

Dane faked another yawn, backstepping into Clifton, who crept alongside the little man until they reached a room, where they both fell inside.

"Well, that was a close one," Clifton said.

"Too close," Dane added. "This was a stupid idea." He lit his bedside candle.

Clifton's stomach growled again. "You got any dinner leftover? I'm starved."

"Gonna havta kiss the hare's foot, I'm afraid."

"Kiss what?"

"It means ya missed the meal so ya get whatchya get." The dwarf tossed a huge section of the loaf of bread onto the table, which Clifton instantly scarfed down.

Between chews, he said, "So what's next?"

"We leave before sunrise and head to Sherwood Forest. It's a two-day journey so we pack only what we need." He frowned.

"What is it?" Clifton asked.

"I'll have to grab coin from Mater's pouch."

"Will she get mad?"

"Of course, she will. Furious. But I'll replace it. That's the least of our concerns."

"What do you mean?"

"Your story checked out, Clifton. The Arrows of Light are in the Sheriff's possession and soon to be in Prince John's. He's challenged Robin Hood to an archery contest, and the archer stands no chance to win against the deceitful Prince. We must help him, lad, to save the kingdom. To save all the kingdoms."

Clifton gulped. "Do you really think we can win?"

Dane shook his head. "Nah, boy. Don't think we

stand a chance."

Chapter Fifteen
Olivia Lovegoode

It was like old times again, trekking through the woods with his good pal Dane, headed on an epic journey, a wondrous adventure. The dwarf pushed through foliage and kicked rocks, grunted his displeasure, and even tried catching critters off the beaten path. Although he appeared more childlike than the wise dwarf from 1485, it was hard to grasp that he and Dane were nearly the same age. Of one thing Clifton was certain: in this timeline, Dane was living, and somehow or another, he planned to keep him that way. He would warn Dane to take precautions or die on Bosworth Field.

Like Marty McFly had tried with Doc Brown.

By predawn, the temperature dropped to its dew point. Between the crowns of the trees, millions of stars glittered in a black velvet sky. Dane's soundless gait led the way with the bone crunch and crackle of dry twigs and dead leaves from Clifton's untrained steps following closely behind.

Dane said, "Tell me more about this hobthrush. What did he say, exactly?"

"Basically, he said he'd been sent by the Sheriff of Nottingham to get the arrows for Prince John. I know how this story goes. I've seen the Robin Hood tale with Mel Gibson, Taron Egerton, with singing men in tights, even the Walt Disney animation where Robin and Maid Marion are foxes and Prince John the Lionheart is an actual cartoon lion and—"

"If'n yer gonna spout out balderdash, hold yer tongue. I've got no time to be wastin' on things that don't make any sense, ya hear?"

Clifton splayed out his hands. "Sorry, man. This is hard for me to believe. Where I come from, Robin Hood's a legend, a story. Someone people talk about for entertainment value, not as a current event."

"It's got me pitchkettled, too, lad, but ya don't hear me talking about woodness."

Clifton stared, puzzled. "And I'm the one spouting balderdash? I literally have no idea what you just said."

"Now, we're even." He turned and continued. "So, if that hob knew of yer whereabouts, then it is safe to say others know, too, and might even know yer here in Griffon Forest now."

Clifton hadn't thought of that. His palms began to sweat.

"I think," Dane said, "it'd be best for me to take the lead on this one and fer you to simply follow. At least until we know more. I'm not sure if I trust ya yet, but you've given no reason not to, so I will. For now.

But, Clifton, do ya think you can move a little more quietly? It's like tip-toeing through Pater's bedroom with a barnacle goose in tow."

With a nod and reddened cheeks, Clifton followed and the two walked in silence—well, as silent as Clifton could manage. He couldn't help thinking about Dane's life as a teenage dwarf. What did mythical creatures do in Medieval times? Dane's dad had been yelling at him for hanging out with the wrong type of people but didn't say what for. Were they harassing local fairies at watering holes? Carving graffiti into Griffon Forest trees? Maybe Dane and his nefarious friends had busted a rope bridge so others couldn't cross the river anymore. Could his dad have been talking about Liv? Doubtful. Apparently, he and Olivia Lovegoode were not on speaking terms. Clifton's mind teemed with possibilities.

"So what do teenage dwarves do? I mean, do you go to school or something?"

"School? Blasted, boy. School is for hufty-tufty dreamers, who don't put food on the table."

"Isn't that your parent's job?"

"Me who?"

"You're, uh, mater and pater. Don't they feed you and clothe you and keep you safe, and stuff?"

With a grunt, Dane replied, "I expect you go to school."

"Unfortunately."

"Yep, hufty-tufty dreamers."

Clifton's fists balled at his sides. "Listen, man, you don't know me—"

Dane shot around and pressed Clifton into a tree. "Aye, I don't. But ya sure do know a lot about me, dontcha, lad?" He released after he felt his point had been made.

Typical Dane, Clifton thought, and with a smirk, he said, "So I guess you'll grow up to be a hunter or something?"

"A hunter?" Dane, annoyed by the boy's question, said nothing, and began to walk. Finally, he answered, "As soon as I'm of age, I'm headed to Romania to join the Royal Dwarf Army and travel the realms of Earth. If I'm lucky, I'll be selected for the Elite DFD Corp."

"What's that?"

"The Dwarves Fighting Dragons Corp. An elite group of the bravest, toughest, meanest, and smartest dwarves in the RDA. Been a Jr. DFD for twenty years now, top of me troop. And lucky for ya, I'm trained for this type of travel."

"Yeah, I feel really lucky right now."

"Bah! Ya don't even know what yer getting into, do ya, lad?"

"Nope, but I bet you're about to tell me."

They crossed a brook over a felled log, not too high, but high enough to make Clifton focus on his steps.

"This hobthrush," Dane said, "he's dangerous. And so are his friends, the bogles. To reach Nottingham, we first pass through dark caves, deep crags, and plush woods, home to both of these malicious creatures. Pranksters, they be. Though some play more deadly than others."

Clifton swallowed hard. "Deadly?"

"Aye. Now stop yer yapping and follow me." Without a word, he marched behind the dwarf. But the snapping of a nearby branch and the voice that spoke through the darkness caught both their attention.

"Yer on private property. Dontcha move or I'll shoot ya both dead."

And without a doubt Clifton knew that Liv had joined their party.

Chapter Sixteen
The Party

"Olivia, it's me, Dane Englewood." He lifted his hands in surrender and Clifton followed suit. "Blasted, girl. Put yer weapon down before ya do something with it ya wish ya hadn't."

"Ya mind yers, dwarf. And this one?" She pushed the bodkin tip into Clifton's chest and his hands lifted even higher. "What's this one, ya got with ya? A human boy? Why he's practically a baby."

"I'm not a baby. I'm practically the same age as him." He pointed to Dane. "Well, in human years."

"Aye, disarm yerself, Liv. Yer acting a fool."

"Yeah, Liv. Put it down."

"Whatcha be talkin' to me fer, *baby*? And who are you, dwarf, to tell me what ta do on me own land?" She stepped into the moonlight. Fiery red hair fell in swooping curls across her shoulders. In her bright green eyes, Clifton saw the kindhearted dwarf he'd met in 1485 hidden inside this brazen girl. "I be the one with the weapon and yer on me property."

In a swift motion, Dane slammed into Liv and pushed her to the ground. Clifton backstepped, out of reach of their grapple. They rolled through leaves and dirt, with Dane overpowering Liv, then Liv overpowering Dane, until she finally found herself pinned face down in the dirt, both of them panting to catch their breath.

"Get off me!" she screamed.

"Not until yer calmed."

"I am calmed!" she screamed louder.

Dane struggled to keep the bucking bronco still, until Liv finally caved, and her breathing slowed.

"You weren't kidding when you said you didn't get along," Clifton said. "It's a wonder how you two ever fall in love."

"Fall in love? With this creature?" Liv said, disgusted. "Why, he's not fit ta hold a candle to."

"Yer no peerless paramour, yerself, Liv." Dane tightened his grip on her. "But unfortunately, this child knows of what he speaks. In other matters at least."

"Then get off me, dwarf, or perhaps yer holding me down out of affection? Is that it, Dane? You've got the romance for me?"

Dane jumped up and wiped his hands on his pants. "Beshrew thee, woman!"

Laughing, Liv stood, and brushed the leaves off her clothes. "Thanks for the tip, child. That had him jumpin' like a June bug."

Arms crossed, Dane glared at Clifton, who didn't think he did anything deserving of the look. "Don't shoot the messenger," Clifton told him.

With a grunt, Dane pushed past Clifton and Liv. "We'd best be on our way, lad. Hava lot of ground to cover before we reach Nottingham."

"Nottingham?" Liv asked. "Whatcha be headed to Nottingham fer? And in the wee hours of the morning. I know. You must be on a secret mission for the DRD?" She burst into laughter.

Dane trudged off and Liv's lively howls followed like an echo. Clifton rushed to keep up, but they were both stopped by Liv, who jumped in their path trying to compose herself. "Please forgive me. The hour is early, and my humor is sometimes inappropriate."

Dane harrumphed, just like his dad. "Our business is our own, dwarf. We need easement through yer property and nothing more."

With a sideways smile, Liv said, "Well, that'll cost ya."

"What?"

"Ya heard me right. And I don't mean coin, dwarf. That's worthless to me."

"Then whatcha want, Liv?"

"Tell me why I should let ya pass. Why're ya going to Nottingham? I know yer pater don't know and I reckon ya want ta keep it that way."

Dane crossed his arms. "Extortion. That's a new low, girl."

The hyperfastidious dwarf turned her sights on Clifton. "Well, since his tongue's tied, ya tell me what's going on in Nottingham or ya can both turn around and head back to where ya came from."

"Ya better stint your clappe, boy."

Clifton looked between the two dwarves, wishing more than anything they were at least friends, for his own protection, if nothing more. “Well, I’m not so sure I’m at liberty to say—”

“Why are ya headed to Nottingham? It’s a simple question, child. And you, Dane Englewood, will not take one step further on my pater’s land or I’ll wake him up and he’ll tell yer pater yer sneaking off in the middle of the night.”

Dane knew he’d been beaten and his shoulders hunched in defeat. “Ya asked for it, Liv. Remember that.” Her smug smile beckoned him to continue. Pointing, he said, “That’s Clifton Chase. He’s not from here or even from this time. We’re on a quest to save Robin Hood and we need to be on our way. There. Now ya know everything. Ya happy, Liv?”

“Everything, Dane? Not likely. First of all, why’s this boy here and where or when exactly is he from if’n he’s not from this time?”

Clifton chimed in. “I’m from a place in the future that hasn’t even been discovered yet.”

“How do ya mean, ‘the future’?”

“Like time-travel. I’m from the twenty-first century. I know it sounds crazy, but I was sent here to help Robin Hood, after this hobthrush showed up in my room and stole some stuff that was pretty important to me for the Sheriff of Nottingham. We’ve got five days to get to Robin Hood and help him out. Otherwise, the whole kingdom will be in big trouble. Maybe even all the kingdoms, right Dane?”

The dwarf nodded. “Aye, lad. Ya speak truth.”

Liv stared wide-eyed from dwarf to boy, waiting for one of them to let her in on the joke. “Oh, this's rich, Dane. Where'd you find this one? Court jester?"

Stone-faced, Dane said, "It was the Arrows of Light that the hob stole from him."

Liv's countenance fell and the whole forest seemed to still. She faced Clifton. "Is this true, boy? You held possession of the Arrow of Light?"

"Arrows," Clifton corrected. "There were three of them."

"Well in that case, I must join yer party."

"Oh, no, ya don't," Dane said. "We're doing just fine on our own."

She got in his face. "Ya know very well, Dane Englewood, that I've spent the past several decades studying the life and languages of the forest, with a particular interest in hobthrush and bogles, perfecting fluency in seventeen different languages and dialects." With her finger flapping in reprimand she added, "Yer an even bigger fool than I thought if ya don't bring me along as yer guide."

Dane's eyes widened, and he gulped hard. "Bloody well seems I don't have an opinion on the matter, so ya might as well get yer things."

With a squeal, Liv hopped into the air before kissing Dane on the cheek and rushing toward her cottage to pack. "Be back in five," she sang over her shoulder before she was out of sight.

Though he thought it went unnoticed, Dane smiled the tiniest of smiles, as he rubbed the spot on his face where Olivia Lovegoode had planted a kiss.

Chapter Seventeen
Stop Dragon

Liv led like a Ranger, pushing both Dane and Clifton to near exhaustion. She insisted they persevere without breaks until she decided the time to stop, "…being the expert in farm and field for these parts."

By midday, the dirt path declined to a small bank where a river sped past, the rapids light. The three ate their lunches quickly and quietly. Clifton stared at the oasis and carefully maneuvered across river rocks to reach the water, where he bent and took a cool drink. Dane rested beneath a shade tree. He leaned against the trunk, tilted his head into his crossed arms, and was sawing wood almost instantly. His snores made Liv laugh. She hung her feet in the cool water enjoying a crisp apple from her satchel.

"We rest fer as long as it takes me to eat this fruit."

Clifton nodded and drank until, satisfied, he laid across the hot rocks to bask in the warm sun. He was almost asleep when he heard, "Careful, you might fall in."

He turned toward the voice in the water. "Pearl. What are you doing here?"

She paddled in the light current, clutching a large boulder. "I'm just checking on you. How are things going?"

Clifton adjusted to block Pearl from Liv's sight; his voice low. "Could be better. Liv has us on a tight watch, like she's a drill sergeant or something. She's taking this really serious."

"It *is* really serious," Pearl added, eyes sparkling.

Her hair floated on the surface in long strands that he wanted to touch all of a sudden. Her lips parted, no moved, and he had this overwhelming desire to kiss her… His face hit the water hard as the rest of him fell into the river. He gasped for air, the cold snatching his breath away, and Pearl ducked as Liv and Dane both shot a glance in their direction. Clifton pushed onto the river rocks, dripping with water, ignoring the dwarves' gaze.

"Ya all right there, lad?" Liv asked. Dane harrumphed and closed his eyes.

Clifton offered a weak wave without a word. Pearl resurfaced, and he stared blankly at her trying to remember the past several moments.

"Clifton! Are you listening to me?" she asked.

He shook his head clear. "What happened?"

"What's the last thing you remember me saying?"

He wiggled his fingers in his ears to fix his hearing. “You were talking?”

Pearl rolled her eyes and let out a huff. “You don’t have in the Silencing Stones. Well, no bother.”

“I don’t carry them, you know, because they’re so special. Like you. And I didn’t think in a million years I’d ever run into you again.... not that I’m upset...it’s the most wonderful thing that could happen to me. I just would’ve carried the stones at all times if I ever thought there was even a chance I’d see you again.”

She called him closer with her pointer finger. He happily obliged. Was she about to kiss him? Eyes closed, he puckered his lips and leaned in, but instead of her soft lips, he felt hard pressure in his head.

“Ouch!” He cupped his ears. “What was that?”

The Silencing Stones. She’d put them in. They acted like hearing aids, only instead of amplifying sound, they silenced Pearl’s magic. Pearl was a young Siren, after all, which meant her insatiable ability to lure men to their deaths hadn’t fully developed...yet. By providing him with Silencing Stones, her charms wouldn’t so easily affect him.

“Thanks,” Clifton said. Embarrassment painted his cheeks as he remembered he had just tried kissing her. “Wait a minute. I didn’t have these when you came to Wickham Park. Why didn’t I fall under your spell then?”

“Mythology is only in books where you are from. Here, myths and legends are born. Our world is closer to the magic’s origins; therefore, you feel my pull stronger in this time, even more so than in the 1400s when we first met.”

He hadn't considered that. This time was like the realms of Middle Earth from the Tolkien books he'd read, not what he was taught in school about the Middle Ages. "Why did all the magic disappear? I mean, where did it go?"

Pearl's eyes lost their sparkle. "The more humanity focuses on building and controlling the world, the less the world speaks to it. This planet contains everything man will ever need, yet he constantly seeks to conquer it and find more, better ways to live. The earth will continue to silence as our kind begins to move deeper into her belly. That is why these creatures are only in your fairytales and storybooks instead of coexisting with mankind as they've done from the beginning. You will see, Clifton, that the longer you are in this time, the more the magic feels like it belongs."

Pearl pushed off the boulder and swam closer. "You know I didn't just come here to check up on you, right?"

Clifton picked up a pebble and tossed it in the rapids. "Kinda figured. What now?"

"Your arrival has spread. News of a boy from another world with the power to wield the Arrows of Light has reached all the realms."

Clifton smirked. "Woah. I sound pretty epic." Pearl's unimpressed expression made him sad. "Listen, Pearl. I know you mean well and I appreciate your warning, but I honestly have a good feeling about this. It's pretty amazing, actually."

"What is?"

Clifton gestured back over his shoulder. “Dane. Alive.” Playing with a reed, he added, “I never thought I’d see him again.”

Pearl smiled sweetly. “You are a good friend, Clifton.”

“You know, I sometimes wonder—”

A large shadow passed over them, bathing the rocks, the river, and the opposite bank in stark gray. Clifton jumped to his feet and stared into the sky. The feathered body of a large bird blocked out the sun as she passed overhead.

“Simurgh!” Clifton called, his eyes trained on the underbelly of the beast. Only something wasn’t right. The feathers appeared rough, scaled even, and the proportions didn’t match those of the Bird of Reason, who had saved him on more than one occasion during his previous adventure.

“Clifton, run,” Pearl said as she plunged into the water and disappeared.

The large creature reached open air and made an arching curve to double back in their direction. Clifton advanced toward the dwarves, who stood staring up into the sky, weapons drawn.

“Is that a…?” Clifton asked as the monster drew near. “A cockatrice?”

And he didn’t need to wait for an answer from them. The dragon’s fire assault told him it clearly was.

Chapter Eighteen Cockatrice

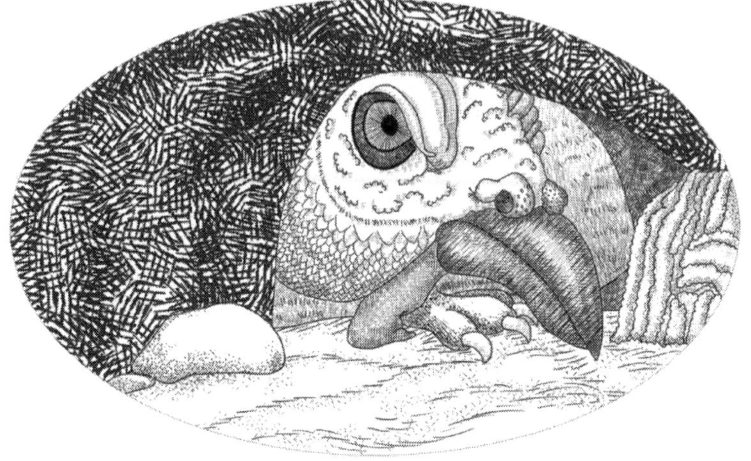

A burst of flames licked their heels as the three travelers ran from the river, the open field, and the cockatrice. The pungent oil that coated the dragon's glands and allowed her to exhale fire stung Clifton's eyes and made them water.

"Keep running," he yelled as he passed the dwarves. "She's coming back around!"

Dane and Liv scurried behind; their soft steps absorbed into the leaf-littered woods. They abandoned the river path they'd so meticulously followed, headed deeper into the forest, and far beneath the dense trees. With an explosive crack, their veil quickly glowed red as the dragon's breath ignited the crowns.

"She's a mean one, ain't she?" Dane said, in short bursts.

"Nonsense. She's a dragon," Liv stated. "Breathing fire's what she does. It's not personal."

"I know that," Dane argued. "Ya don't think I know that? I was merely making light of the situation."

"She's making enough light on her own, dontcha think?" Liv ducked beneath low-hanging limbs and trekked up the side of a dirt shelf. "We need shelter she can't burn. And fast."

"Well, yer the expert in *farm and field*," Dane said sarcastically.

She glared. "I know. Follow me." Liv took off on meaty legs around a bend.

"Course, ya do," he mumbled beneath his breath following after her.

Clifton smirked. Even here, even in the midst of impending doom, the dwarves bickered over any and everything. But the engulfed woodland that burst into a long line of fire wiped the smile off his face. Instantaneous heat pulled the moisture from the air making it difficult to breathe.

"Liv, wait up!" he panted, as he passed Dane.

The little man's eyes widened. Behind him, the flames were crowning, creeping steadily closer—too close for his rump's comfort, to be exact. Embers of ruby red rained down and he sprinted, his legs pumping double-time to keep pace.

They reached Liv, who stood near the entrance of a cavern hewn into the side of a rocky pass. Her outstretched arms held a notched bow and arrow, poised to shoot the cockatrice once it came into view. "Get inside, the lot of ya," she said.

"Oh, no... ya don't," Dane said, bending over to catch his breath.

"No, I don't what?"

Heaving, he continued, "Dontcha be thinkin' yer the hero, woman." He dangled one plump finger in the air to let Liv know his monologue was nowhere near finished.

"Ya stubborn fool," she said, impatiently. "This ain't about who's the hero. It's about the boy and the Arrows of Light and doing whatever needs doing. Dontcha understand?"

"Course it's about the boy and the arrows. I'm jus' sayin' ya don't always have to lead, Liv. Sometimes, ya can follow."

"Oh, is this about ya being the big strong man and me the damsel in distress?"

"Dang it, Liv!"

The dwarves' voices rose into an all-out, knock-down argument that left Clifton near the entrance of the cavern wondering his next move. In the distance, the flapping wings of the cockatrice drew closer. Treetops pushed out in waves as the beast neared.

Clifton peered inside the dark cave, wanting to go in, but unable to see through the pitch. "Uh, guys? Could ya maybe fight later so we don't all die?"

The dwarves stopped, looked at Clifton, and silenced themselves, both realizing they'd lost focus. Liv faced Dane. "Go help the boy."

"Aye," Dane answered, as he moved to the cave entrance. He turned to face Liv. "Dang it, woman. Why do ya always make it difficult?"

"Part of me charm, I s'pose." She smiled sweetly.

The cockatrice screeched, piercing the air, and Clifton covered his ears in spite of the Silencing

Stones that he realized, in that moment, he still wore. The large dragon hovered, wings flapping to hold position. She was monstrous, the size of several school buses clumped together, and still more than sixty feet in the air. Her body was covered in scales that caught the sunlight in iridescent shades of jade and indigo. All things considered she was kind of beautiful, until she flapped her enormous wings to stabilize in an upright position.

Dane stared up, mouth wide, and stature stiff. Liv tightened her grip, lifting the bodkin tip to find her target. The cockatrice expanded her enormous torso and Dane pushed Clifton into the cavern. Liv, seizing opportunity, released the bow and sent her arrow into the soft flesh of the dragon's underbelly. But the arrow bounced off, like hitting rock. Liv back peddled, turned, and ran as the beast blew fire in one long line. Her eyes widened from fear as the flame chased her, burning up everything in its path. Dane stepped out of the cavern, caught hold of her, and pulled Liv into the cave, just before a wall of fire zipped past. The three shimmied back into the cavern illuminated by the dying flame, where the room opened into a wide chamber. The smooth stone floor slanted to several pools of water that rippled as the ground shook.

"Cockatrice must've landed," Dane said.

Clifton peered back around the corner. The dragon tried to push her way in the entrance, but her head was too big to fit inside. Roaring in frustration, she paced on massive quads searching for a way in. He hoped she wasn't that smart. With a final push, she leapt into the air, the sound of her wings diminishing as she flew further away, leaving the land quiet. The crackling fire near the entranceway died down as the oil burned, slowly taking the light.

In the dark, Clifton strained to hear anything else, and nearly had a heart attack when Dane blurted out, "Dang near got blasted!"

"Jeez, Dane. Think you could be any louder?"

"Aye, but why would I wanna do that?"

"Never mind."

"That was a close one," Liv added. "Too close."

Dane ambled to the pools of water, cupped his hands, and cooled his face and the back of his neck. Liv quietly replaced her weapons in their holders.

The dragon gone, Clifton tried to relax, though the near dark cave worked against his nerves. A steady trickle of water replaced the crackling fire. His fingertips brushed the smooth, wet walls. "What is this place?"

"The Limestone Caverns," Liv said.

"Pretty dark in here," he added. "Once that flame burns out, it'll be pitch black. Are we gonna go out the way we came in? Do you think that dragon's waiting for us?"

"Blasted, boy!" Dane said, and even in the growing darkness, Clifton recognized the frustrated scowl that Dane wore so often, so well. "Are you planning to talk the entire time or do ya think you could be quiet for one dang minute?"

"The whole time of what?" Clifton asked.

Then, he noted Liv taking glimmering powder out of three separate pouches she had tied to her waist. It reminded him of the time on his previous adventure in a place called Eze, when Jasper Tudor, the princes' bodyguard, took out his own shimmering dust and chanted a spell. Come to think of it, they were being chased by a dragon then, too.

A bang at the entrance shot the three into overdrive. The fire had died down almost completely and the cockatrice was back. This time, she used her bony head to knock into the opening.

"She's trying to get inside!" Clifton said. "What do we do?"

Liv chanted a spell in a tongue Clifton had never heard before. The words spilled out of her mouth almost visually and made Clifton feel spongy and warm.

"We do nothing, lad," Dane said. "Liv is a gifted pythoness. Let her do what she does best."

"A pythoness?"

"Shut it, lad. Just watch."

As the dragon crumbled the entryway, Liv's lilt lifted and her words carried throughout the cavern. The sponginess Clifton felt bled into the walls and the floors of the cave. They reached the cockatrice, who stopped destroying the limestone and let out bleating cries like a wounded sheep. Liv chanted louder, stronger, until the beast reached its pain threshold, lifted into the air, and flew out of their sight.

No one moved for some time until they all knew the coast was clear. Liv's glowing face had taken on an opaque sheen. Her hands turned up and the dust on the limestone floor lifted with a swirl that formed into three torches, the tips lit, and each torch flew respectively into the hands of Dane, Clifton, and Liv.

"Woah! That was epic," Clifton said.

Liv smiled. "The fastest way to defeat a hard enemy is ta soften 'em."

She winked, and Clifton grinned. So that's why he felt spongey. "That's lit."

Dane huffed. "Yer time affects yer tongue, boy."

"Oh, sorry." He faced Liv and bowed. "What a grand display of magic, me lady."

Liv splayed her hand across her chest to feign surprise. "My, what manners ya have. Seems ya could be teaching some to the dwarf, here."

Clifton said. "How come I never knew you were a pythoness before now?"

Liv looked confused. "Ya didn't need ta know till now, did ya?" Clifton shook his head. "Very well then, seems ya answered yer own question."

Dane harrumphed, Clifton snickered, and Liv gloated.

All was as it should be, until a skittering sound up ahead stole their attention.

Chapter Nineteen
King Orgon King

Scampering feet moved expertly through the dark cavern led by high-pitched chortles that cracked the muck and decay. Quiescent glee bounced off the walls in an invisible tennis match as giggling creatures zipped past, stepping on Clifton's foot, pulling his hair, or yanking his t-shirt hem faster than he could respond. Clifton whipped around, but the mischievous creatures slipped by, dousing their torches out one by one.

His hand disappeared from before his eyes and panic constricted Clifton's throat. He was in the past, in the dark, in a cavern, with some freaky, ghoulish things bouncing around at his expense, evil creatures bent on eating him. Was human a delicacy in this part of the world? Maybe they preferred dwarf.

"Stick close, boy," Dane said. His plump hand curled around Clifton's collar and yanked him over.

"Masked in darkness, cloaked in night," chanted Liv, her voice deep and penetrating. "I call ya forth into the light. Lux Fortem!"

In an instant, a supernatural spotlight shone brilliance from the ceiling to the floor. It split into many lights that struck the creatures, revealed their positions, and spread their shadows like dark copies on the walls behind them.

Hands outstretched, Liv said, "Back to back now, the both of ya," and her stern face gave neither Dane nor Clifton a reason to do otherwise.

The trio stood in a tiny circle, their backs connected, torches raised in the air in a defensive stance, ready to face whatever hostage had overtaken them.

"Hobthrush," Dane whispered. "Maybe hundreds of 'em."

"Is that bad?" Clifton gulped, already knowing the answer.

"Quiet, ya two," Liv said. "They come swift and without good intent. Be ready."

"Whatdya think we're doing standing here, Liv?" Dane asked. "Posing for a paintin'?"

Clifton stifled a laugh that was quickly replaced with fear as a tiny hand gripped the base of his torch and yanked. "What the—"

"They're here," Liv yelled.

And they were. In droves, dozens and dozens of hobthrush, like the one that had appeared in Clifton's closet just a few days earlier, corralling them. Had it only been a few days? Time was so confusing with the linear chain broken. Clifton couldn't remember when yesterday was or if it were today still. He'd have to figure those thoughts out later. Right now, he was fighting this unusually strong fellow for possession of his torch.

"Clifton, hold tight!" Dane said.

He looked over to see both dwarves battling hobs in the same fashion. The room had become a sea of thrush and the three travelers, an island under attack.

Liv's voice thundered above the commotion, "Impetus quiescat!" And the hobthrush froze as statues.

Clifton craned to eye Liv, his face in shock. He had no idea she was such a powerful pythoness. When he'd met her in 1485, she had been a homely housewife, cooking and cleaning and washing. Her pride and joy had been Dropwater, a delicious blend of black licorice and cream, "grown straight from me garden," she'd not forgotten to mention more than a dozen times as he drank. But this girl, Liv, a teenager, was incredibly powerful.

No wonder Dane was afraid of her.

"Let go, my children, go let," a booming voice sounded.

Following the sound to the cave mouth, Clifton spied a grossly deformed hobthrush wearing purple robes that scraped the floor and a crown hewed from bones. In his hairy hand, he held a large scepter that might have been an animal spine, once upon a time. His arms, too long for his frame, hung like twigs on a tree after the leaves have fallen off.

He pushed through the statue of hobs until he reached Clifton and the dwarves. A head higher than Clifton and shoulders higher than the dwarves, his large gut was eye level to Liv and Dane, who tried reverently to look away.

"Why my hobs are statues are hobs my why?"

"Who are ya ta ask?" Liv said, remarkably able to converse with this thing who spoke in backward sentences. Dane reminded him she was fluent in seventeen languages and dialects.

"I am Orgon, King, Orgon am I. Die you will for trespassing for will you die."

Chapter Twenty
Captured

King Orgon waved his hand and the hobs defrosted before their eyes. Quickly, they bound Dane, Clifton, and Liv by their wrists and ankles before they had a chance to struggle or Liv had a chance to pythonate. The horde of hobs dragged them deeper into the cave network, skittering about the trio as if they were three prize heifers from a county fair. Clifton wondered if hobs ate heifer…uh, human, with a side of dwarf…and started to sweat.

The dark cave twisted and turned, the result of underground rivers carving their history in the walls. A musty scent permeated down shimmering halls lit by wall sconces that burned dragon oil, the scent ghastly. Eventually, they exited the tube and stood on a ledge facing dozens of other tubes dead-ending at the circular center of the mountain. Clifton glanced down into a massive expanse that stretched into darkness and out of sight. Above him ran more of the same. Networks of rope from floor to ceiling held buckets that lifted on pulley systems from an unknown source. Rope bridges crisscrossed the entire structure above monster stalagmites pushing up like teeth from the gums of the cavern. More hobs than he could count rushed around pushing wheelbarrows, carrying tools, and hammering stone. They were miners, Clifton figured, of the gold, silver, nickel, and rubies deposited in the walls by the water.

In the center, sat Orgon's throne crafted from the bones of others less fortunate then Clifton and the dwarves. Or so he hoped. A small group of hobs stood waiting, one of whom was unmistakably Hobbie, the creature who'd snuck into Clifton's room and stolen the Arrows of Light. He glared at him, though Hobbie stared at his hairy feet to avoid Clifton's eyes.

The rope bridge before Clifton and the dwarves swung erratically as too many hobs crossed. Clifton broke out into a cold, clammy sweat. The creatures laughed and teased as they passed him, pinching his arm, kicking his shins, and one even tripped him. As he fell, he knocked several of the little demons off the bridge and down the black hole. A part of Clifton felt terrible, hoping they would be okay. The other part figured it served them right for being so mean.

As he was escorted off the bridge and onto the stone platform along with Liv and Dane, Orgon crossed in his slow, dragging pace and sat on the bone throne, which creaked from his weight. Immediately, a few shaky hobthrush presented him with a grayish slop on a flat stone. The King dug in fat fingers, licking the goop off each hair while chewing loudly. Clifton's stomach turned. During the heinous lunchbreak, a hob attendant brushed the King's hair with a comb ribcage of maybe a squirrel or chipmunk, while another placed his fungus feet into a bowl of steaming water to scrub and two others fanned him with enlarged butterfly wings. Clifton wondered what creature they had once belonged to. The whole ordeal twisted Clifton's face in disgust.

Hobbie stood idly by, with no task or grooming instructions on his to-do list. He was either the King's most trusted, loyal servant or in some sort of punishment. The hobthrush still stared at his big, hairy feet purposefully avoiding Clifton's gaze. *Thief. Lowly stool pigeon.* Why, if Orgon knew the truth about his *trusted* hob… Wait a minute. Maybe he didn't know. Maybe King Orgon had no idea Hobbie was a traitor working for Prince John. That's why he was avoiding eye contact with Clifton. It had nothing to do with his feeling bad about stealing the arrows. He didn't want the King to know he was working a side hustle. That must be it! Clifton bet Hobbie would be in big trouble if Orgon knew about his late-night escapades into other times and dimensions.

Clifton cleared his throat. "Excuse me, sire? King Orgon?"

The King turned, annoyed. "What, what?" Mush spilled out of his mouth as the King didn't feel it necessary to finish chewing before speaking.

Clifton's face cringed from his bad manners. "I, uh… I was wondering, do you always let your thrush run freely to unknown places?"

His eyes squinted. "Hobs don't leave, don't leave hobs. Orgon say so, so say Orgon."

“Never?” Clifton said with a smirk, staring at Hobbie.

Orgon stood, flushed. “Never, never. I am King, King am I. You talk no more, more no talk, you.”

Liv grunted. “You are no king.”

Dane quickly added through gritted teeth, “Liv, maybe ya best be quiet and not make things worse.”

“Me, make things worse? Have ya lost yer mind, Dane?”

“No, and don’t plan on losing me head either.” He faced Orgon. “We mean no disrespect, yer highness. We just needed a place to hide from that cockatrice.”

“Lawrence? Lawrence?” Orgon said. “Gentle is he, he is gentle. Why hide, hide why?”

“Cause he looked like he was hungry,” Clifton said beneath his breath.

Orgon sat down and said, “Time to pay trespasses, trespasses pay to time. Plank walking for you. You for walking plank?”

In a flash, hobthrush jumped up and led the trio to the edge of the platform. His feet acting as brakes, Clifton tried to slow the progression, as Dane and Liv did the same. Orgon laughed a throaty bellow that magnified and echoed throughout the eternal chamber. Clifton glanced back at Hobbie, who now looked up with regretful eyes.

“Liv, do something,” Dane shouted.

“Me? Why’s it always me that’s doing something?”

“Cause you’re better at it than I.”

She smiled. “Oh, Dane. That’s the sweetest thing ya ever said to me.”

The dwarf's cheeks burned rose, even in the darkness, and Clifton couldn't believe they were sharing "a moment" in the middle of their death march. He wished he had the Arrows of Light with him. Or Simurgh. He wished she were there to help. But no help was coming. He would have to figure this one out on his own. In a leap of faith, as hobs pressed him to the edge of the platform that led to the plank jutting out like a diving board, Clifton said to Hobbie, "Don't let them do this, Hobbie. You know we need to get the arrows back."

Orgon roared, "Arrows back where? Where back arrows? Hobbie, what meaning? Meaning what, Hobbie?"

Hobbie covered his head and rocked, muttering beneath his breath.

"Answer me," Orgon spouted, spittle flying from his hideous lips. "Me answer!"

Clifton looked from the King to the hobthrush catalyst who'd brought him there. The other hobs jumped up and down, mouths agape in anticipation of the trio's death. Turning his head, he glimpsed Liv and Dane staring at each other, their gaze fixed as if they were the only two creatures in existence. And Clifton closed his eyes as he reached the end of the plank, knowing his next step would be his last. Wishing he were back in his bedroom, playing with Pierce or talking to Justin on the phone. Wishing he had one more breakfast with his family and one more walk home with Ava.

His thoughts were interrupted, not by his plunge to a painful death, but by shaking ground, rattling the entire cavern and filling the chamber with the loudest roar Clifton had ever heard.

Chapter Twenty-one
Monster

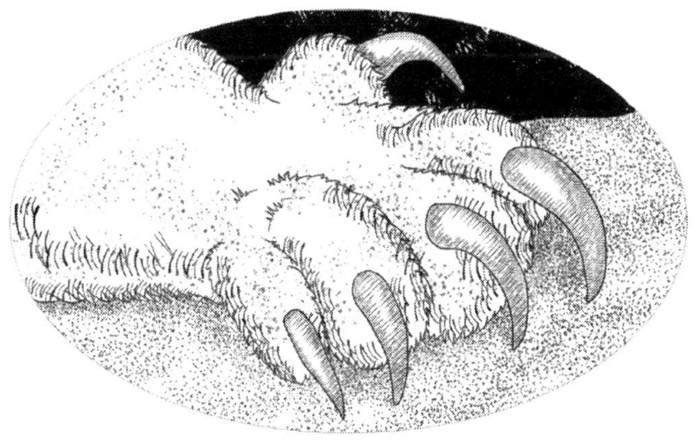

"It's a Tatzelwurm!" Liv screamed.

The ground shook upward, and through the darkness below, a wriggling shape zigzagged along the slick walls of the cavern. Loosened rocks shifted and plunged from the ceiling, sending the room into pandemonium. Clifton had never heard of a tatzelwurm and had no idea what to expect as the monster rushed through points of light that revealed only pieces at a time. He glimpsed spikes growing out of skin like rocks on its back, a tail that ended in a barb of bone whips, a prehistoric head with petal-like mouth, and razor-sharp claws and sickle-like fangs.

Hobthrush lost their mischievous grins, their faces etched in fear as they spun in circles, rushed out through the surrounding cavemouths, or ducked, covered, and prayed.

Even King Orgon wore a look of dread, as he stood and stared into the abyss with the others. Clifton caught his gaze. The King's mouth pulled in a straight line. "You are free, go. Go free, are you." He hefted his robe and shuffled across the nearest rope bridge, his creatures-in-arms scuttling duteously behind.

Liv, Dane, and Clifton were free (if you could call this new run-for-your-life experience *freedom*). No one had thought to unbind them, so they hobbled on bound feet without their hands to balance. Movement was tedious, escape not promising.

"Follow me," Liv said, waddling on her heels.

Dane and Clifton trailed like shadows, though trying to run with one's hands locked behind their back proved to require more balance than either Clifton or Dane could muster. That all changed when the roaring hiss reached the platform, and without meaning to, Clifton peered back for a solitary glance at the *tatzelwurm*.

He immediately wished he hadn't.

The creature's massive head resembled a Jurassic jaguar. Intelligent eyes trained on him and sharp teeth poised to connect with whatever fleshy part of Clifton it could reach from fifty meters away. If that weren't frightening enough, as the beast maneuvered up from the abyss, its body morphed from felid to reptilian, like an anaconda of massive proportions, with bone blades stretching from bulbous plates covering the upper back and shoulders.

Wobbling, Clifton turned, tried to spread his legs for balance, and hopped erratically. He reached the rope bridge and plunged across, using the handrail as bumpers to push off as he bounced like an air hockey puck. A blast of wind struck his back, and as Clifton stepped off the bridge and onto the open ridge of the cavemouth, he turned, his face ashen. Wings pressed out from the monster's shoulder blades, carrying the creature with outstretched paws toward him. Its claws extended into machete blades; the demon's yellow eyes glued on Clifton.

He dropped and rolled, placing enough distance between them for the tatzelwurm to miss its mark. Clifton pushed through the tunnel opening into growing darkness, following Liv and Dane.

"I see a light," Liv said, and Clifton didn't question her.

The three rushed deeper into the mountain on an uphill snaking path. The hissing tatzelwurm followed, crushing the tubular edges as it penetrated with no apparent regard for its own well-being. The cave sloped higher, the space shrunk, and Clifton ducked to escape, hoping the encroachment would slow the beast's progress.

No such luck.

The monster rushed in, a bulldozer in a tunnel, plowing through the walls and gaining on them. Clifton couldn't believe he was about to die in this cave by some creepy cat-snake-worm. But wait a minute. He was with Liv and Dane, the two dwarves who would find him in the forest in 1485. They couldn't die here, so neither would he. Unless, his very presence in 1199 had altered history for the three of them.

Clifton gulped hard, not ready or willing to consider that a possibility.

As the beast drew closer, its roar deafening, they reached what seemed to be a dead end with only a large mouth above, where the light Liv had seen filtered in.

This was it.

The end.

Liv said, "Reserare," and all their bindings fell to the ground.

Clifton kind of wished she'd done that sooner.

"Sorry I couldn't do that sooner, loves," she said. "Wasn't sure of the spell and hoped it'd come back to me memory sooner than later." She smiled sweetly, though Dane and Clifton stared at her, mouths agape. She simply shrugged and notched an arrow. "Gonna stand there like a fish or are ya gonna do something, dwarf?"

"Aye," Dane said, lifting his axe high in the air.

They were fearless to the end, though no match for the beast. Without a weapon, Clifton stood beside them, hoping beyond all hopes for a miracle. The hissing intensified, his hope turned to prayer, and the dwarves resolve grew even stronger.

"We must make it," Clifton whispered. "We will make it." He looked up through the opening above and said, "Simurgh? You out there?"

His answer came in a soaring song that rushed from above like a brilliant white light, growing, intensifying as the music washed down the walls and across the floor, filling every inch of the cave with melody and brightness. The tatzelwurm's roar turned to a shriek, and the fossorial beast was forced back, away from the light as if allergic. It retreated into the darkness until it was gone.

What miracle had saved them? Clifton had a guess, knowing that voice, and he looked up to see the smiling face of his friend Simurgh, the all-knowing bird of reason, with the head of a dog and the body of a great bird.

"Hello, Clifton Chase from the Park of Wickham."

He'd forgotten how beautiful her human face was, violet eyes that sparkled with or without light and a warm smile that reminded him of holidays with family and spending time with friends. Clifton nodded his head in reverence. "Simurgh, you have no idea how happy I am to see you."

"Simurgh?" Liv said in disbelief. "*The* Simurgh?"

With a strong smile, Simurgh said, "Pleased to meet you Liv of Ungorn, and Dane of Drathco."

The dwarves bowed.

"Hey, Simurgh," Clifton said. "If it's not too much trouble, do you think you could get us out of here?"

"As you have asked, it shall be." Her soft wing lowered through the hole above as a wall for them to scale. "And," she added, as the three made their way up, "I will help you get to Sherwood Forest to find Robin Hood."

Chapter Twenty-two Simurgh

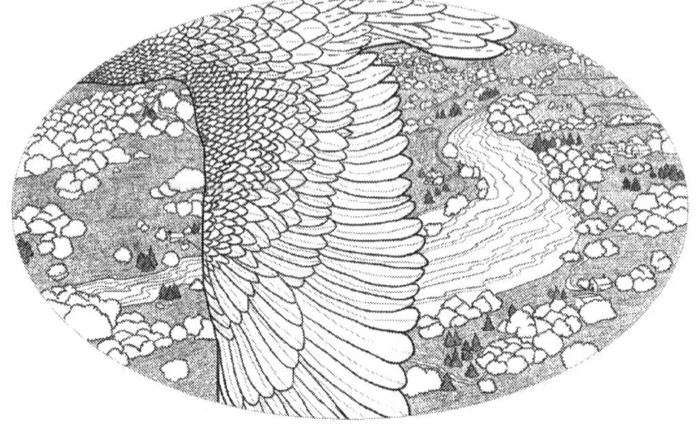

Clifton had forgotten what it felt like to fly.

On the soft down of Simurgh's broad back, he shivered. Currents carried them higher into the chilled air of the stratosphere as the world passed beneath, a canvas of greens and browns and blues. From his vantage point, no lines divided countries or kings.

Dane clasped her feathers in his white-knuckled grip. "Is this to be much longer?" he asked.

"Time is a tricky thing, dwarf," Simurgh answered. "What change does it make for you to know how long the journey will take? You will still be strapped to my broad shoulders until I land." Simurgh belly-laughed, shaking the dwarf, who gripped even tighter.

"Really, Dane," Liv said. "Ya need to be relaxin' nar, not frettin'. Simurgh be the greatest creature in this countryside or any beyond."

"Thank you, My Lady."

"Aye," Liv answered. "There's no safer place in all of the world than where we are right nar."

Clifton smiled. It was like old times again, like the first adventure. He missed the princes, though, Richard and Edward, but they hadn't even been born yet. He smiled. Neither had he, for that matter. This time, the Arrows of Light had chosen him to help Robin Hood. Man, that was hard to wrap his brain around. Might as well be Thor or Captain America or Luke Skywalker. They at least had people to guide them and didn't need the help of a kid from another century. "Simurgh?"

"Yes, young Clifton?"

"Why is Robin Hood taking the challenge with Prince John? I mean, I know he's good and all—"

"Good?" Dane screeched. "Blasted, boy. Good is for the likes of the king's guards. Robin Hood is an anomaly, a brilliant natural."

"Aye, he is," Liv said, dreamily. "And not bad on the eyes, either."

Dane harrumphed and if he could've, he would've crossed his arms and looked away.

"If everyone knows his skills then why would the Prince agree to the challenge?" Clifton continued. "Doesn't he have to, like, set people free or something if he loses?"

"The Sheriff of Nottingham can be quite persuasive," Simurgh said. "The power given to him by the Prince is absolute, and he uses it to take too much in taxes from those who already have too little to survive. Robin Hood takes back only what is needed from Prince John's purse to feed and clothe the poor of

Sherwood. His skills far exceed the Prince's, and although the entire countryside is aware of this truth, the arrogance of the Prince and the Sheriff trump the obvious."

"And with the Arrows of Light," Clifton said, "the Prince is sure to win."

"Indeed, he will win," added Simurgh. "And Robin will be imprisoned or killed by the Sheriff of Nottingham."

Liv frowned. "And there won't be no one lookin' after the people."

"Aye, no one to be their voice to the Prince," Dane added.

Clifton realized in that moment that he never fully understood the story of Robin Hood. In his memory of the Disney cartoon, he hadn't a clue what the fox was doing by taking from the lion prince and giving to the poor. It didn't seem wrong in that context. Here, this illegal choice was a reality that people's very lives depended on. Yet, how immoral was it? On the one hand, it was wrong to steal. On the other, if the prince was stealing first, wasn't Robin retrieving what was stolen? There was no absolute truth to explain it, Clifton thought for the first time. It was both wrong and right.

"Is he wise?" Clifton asked. "Robin Hood?"

"No man is wise in the present, though all are wise in their past," Simurgh said.

Clifton squinted his eyes. "So, that's a no?"

"It depends upon your definition of wisdom. How do you describe wise?" Simurgh asked.

Clifton shrugged. "Like, when I tell him what's happening with the Arrows of Light and Prince John, and especially when he asks who I am and why I'm here to begin with, will he listen to me? Will he take what I say to heart or write me off and go to Nottingham anyway?"

"The answer you receive from Robin Hood is the only one you can expect. You have control only of your words and your task, Clifton. Placing your faith in his reactions will do you no good. Trusting in your message will bring its own reward."

Clifton shook his head and breathed out slowly. Simurgh answered in fortune cookie riddles that left Clifton with more questions than he started with. But in the end, he always found the answer he was looking for, just never in the way he expected.

Liv leaned over. "I hope yer ready to share yer message."

"Why's that?" Clifton asked.

"Cause Robin and his merry men are just below us."

"And they're not fans of dwarves," Dane added.

"Now you tell me," Clifton said.

Simurgh landed softly outside the camp, the trees too dense for her to land elsewhere. The trio climbed her wing to the ground that Dane stared at like a mirage in the desert.

Clifton faced Simurgh. "Thank you. You always seem to appear right when I need you."

"At the right Time, you mean." Her smile grew long.

"Exactly."

Her feathered wing draped his shoulders and she pulled him in close for a hug. "You speak truth, Clifton Chase, and the rest is up to Fate."

Suddenly, his contentment was replaced with worry. The thunder of wings behind him ruffled his hair as Simurgh leapt into the air.

"Blimey!" Dane said. "Think she coulda given a warnin'?"

They watched her trail off, now a small speck in the sky.

"Don't be silly, Dwarf," Liv said with a smile. "She don't be answering to no one."

Clifton took a deep breath and stepped between the white fingers of birch trees along a dirt path. The sweet-scented bark smelled like leather, mixed on the cool breeze with earthen minerals. His mind was so far removed from the world of the twenty-first century, of technology and metal and the smells of hot tar roads and exhaust pipes, that he was energized with a boldness to take on his task and save the day. That was until he rounded the bend, where a group of twenty men faced him, with bows drawn and arrows notched.

Chapter Twenty-three
Legendary

"Don't shoot," Clifton said, his hands lifted in surrender.

The men held fast, staring beyond Clifton to Liv and Dane. He turned his head and found them with their weapons raised, ready to fight back. Two dwarves challenging an army of nearly two dozen.

Through gritted teeth, Clifton said, "What are you guys doing? Lower your weapons."

"Not a chance," Dane said.

"Aye," Liv agreed. "Them first, then we'll follow."

Clifton rolled his eyes, faced the army, and said, "Please, sirs. We mean no harm and I know it doesn't seem like it, but these two are really nice dwarves. I know you guys don't really like dwarves, but I give you my word that they will lower their weapons if you will first."

The men didn't flinch. Neither did the dwarves.

"Okay. I got a better idea," Clifton said. "Why doesn't everyone drop their weapons at the same time, huh? I'll count to three. Come on. We aren't here to fight."

"That's not how it looks to us," a huge man with a dark beard said. His longbow shifted from the dwarves to Clifton. "How'd you find our camp? Did the Prince send you?"

"No. We don't even like the Prince. Honest."

A younger man stepped out from the pack. Rail thin, his wavy blonde hair fell past his shoulders and collected in the hood of his cloak. "Supposed to believe you now, is we? You're more cracked then the pot if you think we'll be taken the word of a strange boy with a strange twist to his tongue."

The Merry Men—though currently, they were more like the Not-So-Merry-Men—inched forward in one accord. They wore layered clothes resembling potato bags in natural shades of brown, tan, and black, with green or blue accents and metal pieces for protection around their legs, arms, and chest. Some were cloaked in hooded garments while others wore leather vests and gauntlets.

"Please," Clifton begged again. "We just need to speak to Robin Hood."

The men snickered. Blondie said, "And why's we gonna tell you where Robin is?"

An old man with a long gray beard ribbed him. Blondie doubled over to absorb the pain. "What this youngin' means is we do not know, that is to say, we know *of* Robin Hood, of course, but not in any *personal* manner."

"Yer lyin'. The lot of ya," Liv said.

"That so?" Blondie inched closer to Liv, to which Dane changed his aim to the boy's head. "On who's authority do you have knowledge that says otherwise?"

"From Simurgh," Liv said. Her eyes lit with a fire that made even Clifton tremble. Knowing what a powerful pythoness she was, he wondered if she weren't conjuring up some silent spell at that very moment.

"Simurgh?" Dark Beard said. "How do you know the great Bird of Reason?"

"Oh, ya know," Dane chided, "by name only. Not in any *personal* manner." He glared at the old man, who stuck his tongue out at the dwarf.

"She's a good friend of ours." Clifton took a brave step forward. "We have to talk to Robin. He's in great danger."

"I told you," said a stout man, who may have been the youngest of them all. "Don't know him."

Blondie grunted. "Already made it clear. There's no one here by that—"

The old man gutted him again. The boy doubled over in agony for a second time, and the old man smiled a toothless grin. "Shut your pie hole, Will Scarlett. These folks ain't as stupid as you look."

The Merry Men laughed, their defenses dropping as the banter between Will and Toothless continued.

Liv saw her chance and wasted no time in their weakness to release her arrow into the crowd. It struck the old man's knapsack, tearing a hole big enough to spill out the contents. Before they could move, she had supernaturally shot through the crowd, notched a second arrow, and was pressing the bodkin tip into Dark Beard's neck. "Dontcha be thinking I missed by accident," she clarified. "Where's Robin?"

Dark Beard squinted and grumbled, "This is why I hate dwarves."

Liv pulled her draw tighter, the bodkin tip digging into the man's flesh. Clifton stepped closer and placed his palm upon the shaft. Liv looked into his eyes and with a very indignant sigh, lowered her bow and replaced the arrow in its quiver. Dane came up alongside her, his own weapon sheathed.

Dark Beard rubbed his neck, checking for blood. "You got five seconds to get out of our camp before we open fire."

"Please," Clifton said. "You don't understand. We can't leave. If Robin Hood isn't warned before the archery tournament—"

"Isn't warned of what, my good man?" Robin asked, as he stepped out from behind a tree, towel in hand.

It was him, the legendary Robin of Loxley. The magnitude of it all hit Clifton like a sea of bricks. He stood in Sherwood Forest with Robin's Merry Men and Robin Hood himself. A black edge ebbed in his vision and slowly forced its way toward the epicenter.

Why was Sherwood Forest spinning?

Robin looked at him curiously, stepped closer, and said something Clifton couldn't make out. The tops of the trees encroached his vision and the ground beneath his feet cupped his body. Robin Hood and the Merry Men encircle him. His eyes closed.

What a wonderful dream, he thought, and the world

went blank.

Part Two:
The Archer

Chapter Twenty-four
Off Guard

When his eyes opened, it took Clifton a minute to remember where he was at. A tarp stretched above him in an off-white shade yellowed by filtered sunlight. He laid on hay bales draped in linen, their sweet scent a tickle in his nose. He tried hard not to sneeze. As he shifted, he noticed two things. First, a pounding knot on the back of his head. Second, how he'd gotten the knot…from slamming into the ground and passing out after meeting the legendary Robin Hood. In person. *Mano-a-mano*.

It all came flooding back.

The front flap of the tent pulled aside, and a young girl stepped in carrying a plate of food and a metal stein filled with water. She was beautiful, with spiral curls, light mocha skin, and dark brown eyes.

"Oh," she said, startled. "You are awake, my lord." She stared inquisitively.

Clifton quickly sat up, ran his fingers through his hair, and wobbled back down.

The girl scooted over in haste. “I would not do that, my lord.” She set the plate and cup on the table beside him. “Just relax. You have a big bruise on the back of your head. It will take time to heal as we have no healers at this camp.” They stared at each other briefly, like long lost souls reunited, until the girl quickly stood. “Are you hungry, my lord?”

“It’s Clifton,” he said, as he sat up, slowly this time. “My friends call me Clifton.” He winced and sucked in a breath. “You don’t have to call me ‘my lord’.”

“Oh, I’m begging your pardon, Clifton.” She curtseyed and he felt his cheeks flush with heat. “My name is Abigail. Abigail Rose. I am Robin’s niece.”

“Nice to meet you.”

She smiled and her cheeks dimpled. “Are you hungry, Clifton?”

“Famished.”

“Well, please eat, then. I will return soon for the crockery and to check on you. When you are feeling up to it, my uncle would like to speak with you.”

Clifton already had a mouth stuffed with bread when he asked, “Thanks. Can you tell me where my friends went?”

“The dwarves? They are a bit…tied up, at the moment.”

He stopped chewing and looked up. “Literally?”

She frowned. “Yes, my lord…uh, Clifton. The men do not like dwarves. They cannot be trusted, as you know.”

Clifton stood, waited a second for his head to stop swimming, and demanded she take him to them.

Her body grew rigid and tense. "As you wish, my lord."

Abigail turned, her skirts whipping around, and exited the tent with Clifton on her heels. The cool air snatched his breath and twigs dug into his bare feet. Maybe he'd moved a little too hastily and could've taken a moment to grab shoes and a cloak.

Too late now.

The Merry Men were clumped in groups talking, sleeping, eating, and drinking. About a dozen linen tents lined the camp. Some were sewn with pieces of leather at the seams. Others had multi-colored panels made of hemp or felt, with separate tops that extended out above the edges, like medieval gutters. Clifton assumed the temporary housing was water resistant, but not waterproof, wondering if they coated the materials with oils from plants or animals, or both, as he passed.

At the end of the lane stood a plain linen tent grounded by ropes tied to pegs. As he neared, the flap pushed opened and a man exited. He was lean and athletic in build with a manicured beard that jutted off his pointy chin. A triangular hat covered his smooth, straight hair, and his layered clothing fit his form, sewn from natural materials in natural shades.

"The boy awakens," Robin said. "How are you feeling, son? Hit your head pretty hard when you fell."

"I'm fine. Where are my friends?"

Robin laughed, a belly rumble. "Now, is that a way to address someone who has done nothing but help you? Didn't my men take good care of you, give you shelter and a bed, and my niece, Abigail, did she not feed you and offer you drink?"

"Yes, sir. Thank you for your hospitality. I'm actually a big fan of yours, believe it or not. This is a bit surreal, to be honest. But my fanboying will have to wait. Those dwarves have risked their lives to come here to save *yours*."

"Nonsense. Dwarves think only of their own hides, son, a truth you'll find benefits you the faster you take hold." He turned to head back into his tent.

The memory of Dane jumping in front of him to take the deadly arrow in Clifton's place crossed his mind and anger flooded him. "You're wrong, sir."

Robin turned. "Am I now?"

"Yes. And you're headed for big trouble. That archery competition with Prince John is a trap."

"And how might you know such things? Only a boy."

"What does age have to do with anything? If you think because you're older, that makes you wiser, you're actually pretty dumb."

What was he doing? He was insulting the greatest archer of all time!

Robin phooeyed him, crossed Clifton's path, and headed outside the circle of tents. Clifton scurried behind, tailed by Abigail. He was not letting the man get off that easily, legend or not. Their procession caught the attention of the Merry Men, who jumped up to join the parade. Robin stopped, retrieved an arrow from the quiver on his back, and took aim on a target Clifton could barely make out, nearly three-hundred yards away. Robin released, and the arrow sped through the air like a lightning bolt, slamming into the bull's eye as if drawn by a magnet.

Clifton felt his knees quake. He had just watched Robin of Loxley shoot an arrow into a target! "This is the sickest moment of my life," he whispered.

Robin smirked, as he notched a second arrow. "I am pretty confident it is the Prince who cannot win."

Clifton composed himself. "Normally, yes. But according to Simurgh—"

"You have conversed with Simurgh? How?"

Clifton swallowed hard, forced himself to focus on his task. "She's an old friend. She helped me once before to save two princes in another time. The Arrows of Light, the ones made from her feathers, they chose me to help you."

Robin released his draw, and the air separated for the second arrow to slice through the first, splintering from the impact. He faced Clifton whose stern expression spoke more than he ever could. "Tell me more."

"Not until you free my friends."

Robin laughed again. "You are not in charge here, son."

"Neither are you."

Robin and the Merry Men turned their gaze upon Clifton Chase, who stood firm, though trembling inside and ready to run. "You know of the arrow's power, don't you, sir?"

"Yes," Robin said. He held eyes with Clifton a moment longer, before he faced the boy with the blonde hair. "Will, go and get this boy's friends."

Will turned—Clifton screamed inside, knowing he was the infamous Will Scarlet from all the stories and movies on Robin Hood and his Merry Men—and blondie disappeared back toward camp.

"Now," Robin continued, as he stepped into Clifton's space. "Tell me why you are here, truly."

"The Arrows of Light came into my possession a while back. They've been in my family for a long time, but I've just discovered them. A few nights ago, a thrush named Hobbie stole them from my closet after he told me his master, the Sheriff of Nottingham, had sent him on a quest to get the arrows so Prince John could challenge you to an archery contest. The only problem, sir, is that you are no match for those arrows."

Robin puffed out his chest. "I am the greatest marksman in the world, I'll have you know."

"Believe me, the legends of your skill are still told a thousand years from now."

"How could you know such a thing?"

"You're not gonna believe me and it doesn't matter."

Robin stepped even closer, his stature stiff and towering. "Try me, son."

"Get yer hands off me!" Liv said.

Clifton turned to see his friends dragged over by Will Scarlett, hands tied behind their backs.

"Untie them," Clifton demanded.

"And what if I don't?" Robin asked.

What if he didn't? What could Clifton do, honestly? He stood in a forest sometime in the eleventh century with mythical creatures and a legend from childhood storybooks.

That was it!

"If you don't, your legend will end here. You will be forever known as Robin of Loxley, the peasant who was defeated by the great Prince John. The people you protect will be abandoned and left to rot in Nottingham prisons, to starve in their homes after they are overtaxed to bankruptcy. The songs they sing about Robin Hood will be filled with despair, hopelessness, and pity, all because you wouldn't listen, remembered only as man defeated by a guy who had to cheat to win." Clifton took a brave step forward. "Now, release my friends."

Robin smiled, and Clifton stood his ground, his palms sweating.

After a moment, Robin clapped a hand on Clifton's shoulder and said, "My boy, your words were spoken as a true friend and hero. Prince John will not gain the upper hand, as we will attack at dawn to retrieve the Arrows of Light. Thank you for your service."

Clifton relaxed, and was about to thank Robin Hood in return, when the famous archer pointed to the old man and said, "Sir Much, take these three prisoners to my tent until the men and I return."

Clifton's jaw dropped as his hands were tied behind his back. "Prisoners? But I thought—"

"Thank you for your warning, Master Chase. I will let you know when I have won."

Robin and his Merry Men jumped on their horses to, presumably, retrieve the arrows from Prince John, as Sir Much led him and the dwarves back to Robin's tent, the camp completely abandoned.

Chapter Twenty-five
Injustice

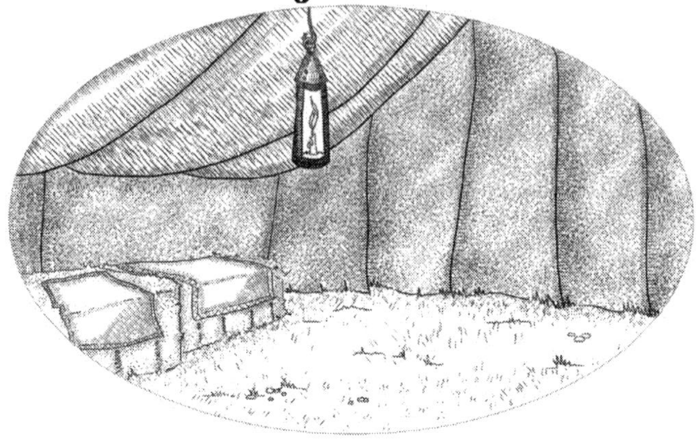

"Enjoy your stay," Sir Much cackled through a toothless grin. He stepped outside the tent, allowing the flap time to close—which ironically now mirrored his gumline—then told the guards stationed out front to "not let them swine or that boy out, no matter what, at all costs," in a voice loud enough for his captive to hear.

"Well, this really stinks." Clifton tugged at the twine bound round his wrists. He actually thought his efforts tightened the rope instead of helping his cause.

"Aye," Dane agreed. "You and yer big trap. Got us sucked into this mess."

"Me? You're blaming this on me?" Dane, who sat across from him, back to back with Liv, nodded. "I was trying to help *you*, man."

"And a lotta good ya did, lad. Now we're all stuck in this camp tied up like pigs."

"Swine," Clifton corrected in sarcasm. "I believe the old man called you swine."

"Why ya little..." Dane struggled to get free in such a frenzy, Clifton backed away, like he would if he'd passed a barking dog tied to a doghouse.

"Honestly, the two of ya, bickerin' on like any of it matters," Liv said. "Who cares why we're here or who's to blame? By my troth, if ya don't start workin' together instead of workin' backward, blaming one another, nothin's gonna change, and we'll be stuck in this blasted tent till they come back to kill us."

Once again, Liv's words of wisdom rang true. Dane harrumphed his displeasure but stopped his struggle.

"So, what do you suggest we do, Liv?" Clifton asked, as he sat on the edge of a straw bale covered in cloth.

"I suggest we start thinkin' clearly. Try and find somethin' from days past to help in our situation nar."

"Come again?" Dane asked.

Liv squinted her eyes and peered sideways over her shoulder, in an awkward position to try and face them both. "Really, dwarf. From you? I'm surprised." She flipped her hair back from her eyes and continued. "Dwarves have been mistreated fer centuries. No matter the rulers or the kingdoms, the blame fer much of the land's misfortunes fall upon the small, yet broad shoulders of our people. We've lost land and family and heirlooms to all degree of creature and men. We can't change our past, Dane, nor what injustices we've endured. We can only find ways ta fix them from becomin' our future. These stories passed to us by the elders, they can turn tragedy to victory. They can make our future clear. Do ya understand nar, Dane?"

Dane's eyes brimmed with tears. "Aye, me lady. I can't believe it took me this long to see it, but I understand me future just fine." His fingers laced around hers behind his back.

"Is that true, dwarf?"

"Aye."

The two dwarves leaned so their temples touched. Clifton could almost hear the violins and cellos soaring in the background, like he was in some epic fantasy film that sidestepped a romantic moment, to which he quickly interrupted, "I, on the other hand, have no idea what you guys are talking about."

Liv looked up with a small smile that curved the edges of her lips. Dane's expression berated Clifton for interrupting their special moment.

"Our people have always been industrious and practical," Liv continued. "Perhaps, a bit gruff, as well, with a knack for finding gems and gold, but our hard work earned us our riches. Our industrious nature built our world. The dwarves of Griffon Forest grew great in numbers, and though we lived and worked in peace, mindin' our own business, those in the surroundin' lands grew envious and fearful of us."

"Like the English in the Battle of Stamford Bridge," Dane added, his face solemn.

"Aye," Liv agreed, as a tear escaped her eye.

"I've never heard of that battle," Clifton said. "What happened?"

"Treachery. Betrayal. Thievery," Dane said. "King Harold Godwinson led the English armies against Norse invaders in the year of our Lord, ten-sixty-six. He created a pact with me family line, the dwarves of Englewood, that we would fight together, using the weapons forged in dwarf fires, being they are much stronger and sharper than any swords forged by men. The King promised to split the treasure with our people in return fer our loyalty.

"The Norse armies, under the leadership of King Hardrada, reached our shores under the cloak of night, but the dwarves were waiting for them. Alongside the English, our ancestors attacked the unsuspecting Norse, burned their ships to ash, and plundered their gold. But King Godwinson broke his word and kept the spoils fer only England. When word reached the Norse King of the battle, King Godwinson swore it was the dwarf army who had ambushed his men, and the English soldiers had not taken part in the battle 'tall."

"Our villages," Liv added, "were burned to the ground by the Norse. Men, women, and children slaughtered in their homes while they slept, forced to run for their lives leaving behind all they owned. All they'd built with their own hands." More tears fell as Liv grew silent.

"We were betrayed, Clifton, by the very men whose camp we sit in now," Dane said. "That's why they hate us. Not fer anything we did, but cause we remind them of their own betrayal, their own cowardice." He motioned toward Liv with his head. "We both lost loved ones in that war. Believe me, the only reason we're here now is because of you, Clifton."

"Why me?"

"The Arrows of Light chose ya, love," Liv said. "And if that choice brings us back into the realm of men, perhaps there's a reason greater than ourselves orchestratin' it." She squeezed Dane's hand. "Maybe it's time we stop pretending what we feel ain't real."

"Couldn't of said it better meself, my lady."

Clifton stewed in silence, awed by the responsibility placed on his shoulders. How could he help, tied up in a tent, when Robin Hood walked unarmed into the lion's den? He tugged at his bindings again, scraped across the cloth covered hay bale, until he found the knot in his rope. "We need to get out of here."

Dane and Liv gawked, as if forgetting he sat across from them. "I'm all ears," Dane said. "How do ya propose escape?"

"I'm not sure. Liv, can you use your hands well enough to untie Dane's or my cord?"

"I'm afraid not. The square knot is too tight, and me hands be too small to tug against it from this angle."

"What about magic? Don't you have an incantation for this or something?"

"Magic comes with a cost, and in this particular moment, the cost outweighs the charm."

Was she serious? Picking and choosing when to cast spells at her own whim? Left to his own devices, Clifton scanned the room. Nothing but mismatched cloth draped from the ceiling and across the many wood and hay pilings scattered throughout. A lantern hung from a cord that sliced the space. They could try to burn through the bindings, though that could prove disastrous if it didn't work out.

A loud crash against the tent caught their attention, as one of the guards was pinned to it by an arrow.

"We're under attack!" someone outside yelled.

"Quick," Clifton said. "I have an idea, but I don't know if it's gonna work or not."

"Great," Dane said. "Let's hear it."

"We need to knock that lantern to the hay bale and set it on fire so we can burn through the tent and run out of here."

"Are ya crazy, lad? What if'n the whole place burns to the ground, and takes us with it?"

Clifton shrugged. "Well, I bet our bindings would burn off that way, too."

Chapter Twenty-six
Unexpected Guest

Dane shook his head and Liv nodded. On three, Clifton launched into the lantern, knocking it to the hay bale, where it broke and spread the whale oil. The dry grass caught easily and fed the fire, which jumped to a hanging panel. The three watched its progressive climb, devouring everything in its path. Clifton hadn't known what to expect, but this sure wasn't it. He quickly wondered if he'd made a mistake as the entire tent wall went up in flames.

"Well this was a dumb idea," Dane pointed out.

The three stood pinned in the center of the tent. Smoke plumed thick and noxious. Outside, the remaining men shouted as arrows flew in through the hemp walls, one wedging into the hay bale between Clifton's legs. That was close. Actually, it was perfect. Using his knees, he rocked the arrow until it loosened. He stood, turned around, awkwardly yanked it free, and handed it to Liv. "Can you use the bodkin tip to slice through your bindings? My hands are too big."

"Aye," she said. She rubbed the arrowhead back and forth, trying to gain purchase to use the tip. The fire had spread to the ceiling, climbing across at record speed.

"Take yer time, me lady," Dane said, as sweat and smoke poured into his eyes.

"Shut it, dwarf. This ain't easy." She gave a small gasp and her bindings fell, followed by Dane's. "Yer turn, love."

Clifton closed his eyes tight as she tugged and pulled at the twine until it snapped and his hands broke free. He rubbed his wrists, red and irritated, then took the arrow back. He covered his face with his arm to block the smoke. "Follow me."

He steered them to what seemed to be the back of the tent, in the direction he believed to lead away from the attackers and the fire. Large pegs held the tent in place, and though they were able to lift the tarp a few inches, the thick smoke labored their breathing and they had to stop.

"What'll we do now?" Liv asked.

"Dontcha know any other spells?"

"Nothing comes to mind."

"Really, Liv. You've got the memory of a fruit fly. Ya should carry a book with ya, or something."

"Aw, shove it, dwarf. Ya wouldn't have gotten this far without me and ya know it."

"True, but if'n we die here, will that matter much?"

Liv let out a tiny scream of frustration.

The tent rapidly burned as the flame licked the first hemp walls, then the support beam, the ceiling, and crept down the other two sides. It began to collapse on itself in the corner where the fire had originated. The heat was intense. Clifton thought his skin was melting off. Soon, the whole place would be up in smoke and flame, and unless a miracle happened, they would be too.

Then Clifton noticed something. Beyond the crackle of fire, it seemed quiet, as if the attack no longer raged outside. "Do you guys hear that?"

"Hear what?" Liv asked through her shirtsleeve. "All I hear is roaring flames."

"Aye. Gonna hear each other dying, soon, and that'll be it," added Dane.

"That's what I'm saying," Clifton added. "I don't hear anyone fighting anymore."

As if eavesdropping, someone threw buckets of water against the burning tent. The water hit the flame like an angry soul sighing followed by a long sizzle and crackling of still burning hemp. A knife blade sliced through the compromised cloth to make an opening for a face to poke through. A face identical to Dane. Like Dane when he'd met him in 1485.

"Oh, *chaff*," Dane mumbled.

"Dane Drathco Englewood," the dwarf bellowed.

"Hello, Pater."

"Boy, yer in a world of trouble."

"I know that. I'm stuck inside a burning tent."

"That'll be the least of yer worries once I'm through with ya."

Liv stared at her feet. Drathco addressed her next. "And you, Olivia Lovegoode... I cannot believe my eyes. What were ya thinking, following me son on one of his crazy, mindless adventures? What be yer mater's thoughts on this?"

"She knows not, sir."

"I see."

"Uh, excuse me," Clifton said. "I get it that you're pretty ticked off and very disappointed, but could we save the lecture for after we're out of the burning, smoke-filled tent?"

Drathco's eyes bugged. "Human, who in mid-Earth do ya think ya are?"

"Clifton Chase, sir. And forgive my rudeness. It's hard to breathe or think, and it's hot as the sun in here."

"I see." Drathco pulled back from the hole he'd made. After a few seconds, the tent tore and fell on both sides to reveal the sky, fresh air, and the face of what had to be an ogre, who opened his mouth to spit out a gush of water and extinguish the remaining flame.

Clifton, Dane, and Liv braced for the shower that drenched them from head to toe. It smelled like week old swamp water and stiffened their clothes and hair.

"Disgusting!" Clifton shouted, shaking off slime.

Liv looked up with a warm smile and said, "We thank ya completely fer ya service, ogre. You've saved our lives."

The ogre's face twisted into what Clifton believed to be a smile. He and Dane cringed. The creature's yellowed teeth hung crooked, like windows in an abandoned house. Hairs sprung sparsely on his chin, chest, and protruding belly, through skin the color of rotting hamburger meat. Liv elbowed Dane as she curtsied.

"Oh, yes, sir ogre," Dane said as he bowed and motioned for Clifton to follow suite. "Yer generosity is unforgettable."

"As is your smell," Clifton mumbled. Dane gave him a dirty look.

"Thank ya, Piesaval," Drathco said to the ogre. "We are in yer debt. Please let us know when and how our services are needed for repayment."

The ogre grunted, farted, and turned to leave. His knuckles scraped the ground as he left in a skimpy loincloth that showed more than Clifton cared to see. He would never get that image out of his head.

"Now," Drathco said. "The three of ya catch a drink and then be ready to talk about why yer here in a human camp with a boy not from this time."

"How do you know that?" Clifton asked. "How do you know I'm not from a different region or province something where we talk and look different?" He tried to pose as if he was a regular from the eleventh century.

Drathco's eyes sharpened into laser pointers upon Clifton. "I have lived a thousand years in this land and never seen the likes of you. Neither yer mannerisms nor yer words ring of this time, no matter how many layers of me son's clothes ya disguise yerself in."

"Pater," Dane said, as he stepped closer. "Let me explain."

"Aye, ya *will* explain. Those be the Merry Men of Robin Hood who captured you and attacked us. Now it looks like we've attacked them first."

"You didn't?" Clifton asked.

As he shook his head in disgust, Drathco said, "See, these are the thoughts of humans and why we don't trust them. Not any of them! Ya assume dead men are innocent men because dwarves' hands are red with blood."

"No, I assume you killed them, but…I didn't mean you are to blame for it."

"Of course, we're not. They captured me son and I simply came to retrieve him, and you too, Miss Lovegoode. But not you, boy. And these men would not listen to me query, nor acknowledge me son's capture. They drew the first arrow and we simply defended our own to retrieve what was ours." He stepped closer to Clifton. "Why are ya here, boy? Why are ya with me son? What is it ya want?"

"Pater, it's not his fault—"

"I was not speaking to ya, dwarf! Nor will I be told where to place fault. It's always on him, on his kind, on the humans that blame falls. They are always the ones with cause."

"Not me," Clifton said. "That's where you're wrong. I came here to help." Drathco took in a breath to speak, but Clifton put his hand in the air to stop him. "My turn to talk. I'm terribly sorry for whatever has happened to your people. Dane and Liv told me some of the history, but I'm sure it's much darker than that. It wasn't right what those men did to the dwarves."

Drathco stared sternly, sizing up the boy's words for truth or lie.

"The only way we're gonna win is by working together. Your son taught me that lesson. And Olivia. Together, as friends, we can conquer anything." Clifton took a brave step forward. "You seem like a great warrior, sir, yet your judgments are based off a past that can't be changed. The future, though, that's in all our hands. Together."

"Yer lecturing me, child?"

Clifton shrugged. "I'm just trying to help you see a different way, that's all."

"Why are ya here?"

"To help the people. To help Robin Hood."

"And what business is it of yers what happens to the people or the Hood?"

"Pater, Clifton is on a quest to retrieve things stolen from him by the Sheriff of Nottingham."

Drathco's eyes lit up as his posture straightened. "The Prince is his enemy?"

"Aye."

"Tell me, boy," Drathco said to Clifton, "what has the Sheriff of Nottingham taken from ya? What could ya possibly possess that he and Prince John would desire?"

"The Arrows of Light, sir." Clifton took his waterskin and drank. Cool water ran out from the sides of his mouth as it quenched his thirst. He wiped his lips dry.

Drathco stared in disbelief, from Clifton to Dane to Liv. His men, too, stopped to look at the ordinary boy who supposedly possessed the extraordinary. A smile crept from one end of his mouth to the other, as Drathco said, "Well an enemy of me enemy, is me friend. Come, boy. Ya may be more valuable than I'd thought." He nodded to his men and two of them grabbed a hold of Clifton on either side.

Dane said, "What are ya doing, Pater? Ya heard him. He's on our side."

Liv covered her mouth and nose and shook her head.

Drathco seethed, "He will face the Dwarf Council and be tried for his thievery. Those arrows do not belong to him. They are dwarf property. And yer a fool for trustin' a word he says."

He turned and his men followed. Clifton fought the best he could, but the little men's strength in number overpowered him. Liv and Dane, led to ponies, watched in horror as their friend screamed for release while dwarves dragged him through the sand, ignoring his pleas.

Chapter Twenty-seven
Dwarf Council

He never would have noticed the entrance if the dwarves had not led him in. The mountain stretched forever in both directions butted up against the long grasses of a valley. Taller than twenty ogres stacked on each other's shoulders, the granite wall sparkled in the bright sunshine cascading down from a clear blue sky. Exhaustion hit as he trudged through the grass to the dead end of a massive stone wall too sleek to climb and too wide to walk around in less than a week's time.

Until Drathco spoke.

"Wayward winds and granite stone, protectors of the dwarf king's home. Reveal yerself and light the way, for dwarves are back and here to stay."

The ground shook and rocks crumbled as a façade wall slid open to reveal an entryway in the mountain. Drathco and his men led the group, followed by Dane and Liv on pony. Clifton felt a hard shove from behind followed by, “Move, human,” letting him know his place in the processional.

When they entered, a dull clambering rang out as dwarves hammered the walls of the chamber that sloped down on a single pass. It spanned across an abyss enveloped in darkness. Dwarves hung on ropes attached to cranes to reach the gems dotting the granite. Behind him, the stone door slid back into place as if it had not been moved by magic. Although scared, Clifton drew wonderment from his surroundings.

They crossed the massive room to a hollow tube that led further into the mountain. Openings on all sides revealed more of the same with dwarves carrying buckets of stones, food trays, and hot water, probably like any other day. As they walked, Drathco and his dwarves-in-arms went off in one direction while Clifton continued to another chamber with his captors. He looked to Liv and Dane for help or direction but met only sad eyes. He was on his own, for now. A curve led to what looked to be a holding cell, where a brownie with teeth like a great white shark snapped at him. Clifton questioned the integrity of the bars, the only things keeping this creature from eating him.

“Get in,” said a black-bearded dwarf as he nudged Clifton into a separate cell beside the brownie.

Clifton complied or rather tripped over his own feet at the nudge and fell into the cell. The door locked behind him. He jumped up and grabbed the bars. “Please, you don’t understand. Robin Hood is in trouble and needs help.”

The dwarf banged his spear into the iron bars and said, “Human problems have no business in the dwarves' mountain. Wait here until the council is prepared."

The dwarf left and Clifton turned around. He could sit on the stone floor or stand. He chose to sit against the wall, as far from the snapping brownie as possible, trying not to cry. What a disaster! Nothing had panned out like he'd planned. Robin Hood had treated him like a dumb kid with no clue, Dane's dad thought him a thief, and this brownie wanted Clifton as his afternoon snack. He placed his head in his hands. How would he ever get out of this?

A voice cleared their throat and Clifton looked up. Liv stood before him. "How ya holding up, love?"

He wiped his face dry and stood. "Not good. What am I gonna do?"

"I don't know. The Dwarf Council is the final word in all dwarfish affairs. They hold yer fate. There is nothing that can be done."

Fear ramped his heart to double-time and a sheen of sweat coated his skin.

"Dane is with his pater, pleadin' with him ta letcha go. All ya can do nar is focus on what brought ya here and have faith that it won't letcha down." She offered a small smile and Clifton nodded.

Guards entered the room, and Liv stepped aside.

"The Dwarf Council is called to order," said the same dwarf who'd locked him up.

"Let him go, Marmoth. He's done nothin' wrong," Liv pleaded.

"You'd be wise to stay out of this, girl. It don't concern ya."

"It does concern me. It concerns all of us, but yer too thickskulled and dimwitted to know when a matter stares ya right in the face."

Marmoth's skin turned red as he stepped close to Liv. "You'd best be watching yer tone, missy."

Liv stepped even closer. "Or what, Marmoth? Whatchya gonna do?"

They stared for a moment, until Marmoth broke away. "I have no time for children." He pointed to Clifton. "Take him to the council."

Two dwarves led Clifton on either side down the hall, through the mountain, and to another room. It opened into a downward slope of carved rows where dwarves sat. The rows faced an open space with a single rock-hewed chair, where the dwarf guards led Clifton. A high tower, positioned in the center of the room, was filled with dwarves wearing red robes and red pointed hats. In the middle sat Drathco in gold robes with a gold pointed hat embedded with jewels from the very walls of the mountain.

The room silenced as Drathco stood. "Clifton Chase from the Park of Wickham, yer charged with thievery of the highest order. What have ya to say for yerself?"

In the pin-drop-silence, all eyes affixed upon the boy from another time and place, Clifton gulped hard. He stared back, mustering the strength he needed to open his mouth. "I didn't steal anything. I've already told you why I'm here."

"But," interrupted a council member, a gray-bearded dwarf who had to be older than dirt, "ya stole the Arrows of Light, didn't ya, boy?"

"No, sir."

"Liar!" said another council member.

"He's lying," echoed another.

The room erupted into murmurs and accusations as the dwarves muttered amongst themselves.

"I'm not a liar," Clifton yelled, and the room silenced at his fearlessness. "I am here because the Arrows of Light chose me to be here. I am an enemy of the Prince and a friend to those who support Robin of Loxley. He's in trouble. He's going up against an evil man who holds great power in the arrows. A friend told me why I'm here and I trust her, because she is the great bird of reason and knows both Time and Wisdom."

A council member stood, small-statured, even among dwarves, and said, "Ya know of Simurgh?"

Clifton nodded. "She is part of the reason why I'm here."

Dane stepped out of the circle to stand near Clifton. "She brought us to Robin Hood, to help him, warn him that the arrows were with the Sheriff of Nottingham, like Clifton said."

"The Sheriff's hobthrush stole them from my bedroom closet. If Prince John uses them against Robin Hood, he will win the archery competition and the people will have no defender, no voice. And if Prince John rules Nottingham without any resistance, his power fueled by the arrows will give him the ability to take over your land, too, to enslave your people. He will become unstoppable."

"Aye," Liv added, as she stood beside Dane. "The arrows offer the holder protection and long life, traits we do not wish to see Prince John acquire."

Clifton looked up at Drathco and begged, "Please, King Drathco. I need to help Robin. It's why I'm here. I'm afraid if I fail, the whole world will suffer. Even those in my own time."

Drathco stared as long as he needed before he turned to the Dwarf Council for deliberation. Clifton sweated while he waited, grateful for Dane and Liv, who stood beside him.

Finally, the council quieted, and Drathco spoke. "Ya plead a good story, lad, and we believe ya, Clifton Chase of Wickham Park. Yer heart is strong like a dwarf's and yer courage is felt. The Dwarf Council finds ya not guilty of thievery and yer released."

"Thank you, your Highness," Clifton said. "You won't regret—"

"I wasn't finished," he seethed. "Yer released from our care and will return to yer time immediately."

"What? I can't go yet. I don't even know how to get home from here."

"We will retrieve *our* Arrows of Light from the Prince. The chimera will take ya home. Guards, bring this boy to the beast, then prepare to attack Castle Rock."

Clifton stood in silent disbelief. What should have been good news turned into utter disappointment and sheer horror.

Chapter Twenty-eight
Bestiaries

Two dwarf guards led Clifton through the mountain to a valley white with moonlight. A wooden stable housed many creatures, mostly ponies and a horse or two, but also mythical beasts Clifton had only read about in storybooks. A hircocervus—a half-deer, half-goat being—contentedly ate straw and barely looked up as he passed. In the adjoining stall, stood an oversized salamander with a charcoal black body spotted yellow. The only noticeable difference between this amphibian and the ones from back home were the dragonfly-style wings growing out of its smooth back.

The neighboring stable sheltered larger creatures and Clifton wondered if he'd stumbled upon a secret menagerie. A low growl, like a leopard, emanated from the darkness in the second stall. Two glowing eyes peered out.

"Woah, there," said the dwarf with a sideways gait. They crept cautiously alongside the greater of the two stables. "It's all right, Dalestrom. We're just passing through. No need to get excited."

The roar that followed lifted the hairs on Clifton's neck. Put a hop in the two dwarves' steps, too. The animal inside swiped a massive paw through the opening, and Clifton feared the wood wouldn't be sufficient to keep this monster back.

"What's wrong with Dalestrom?" asked the other dwarf, a skinny man with red bumps all over his face.

"Think maybe he's hungry?"

"Could be. Ya can keep this creature on yer own, eh? I'll go grab a squirrel or two?"

"By creature," Clifton interjected, "I can only hope you're not talking about me, but rather that monstrous thing that is trying to eat us, right?"

"Shut up, lad," said the first dwarf. "Dalestrom be no monster. He's misunderstood, 'tall. A pussycat, really."

"More like a large spotted one that can move at great speeds, should it find a way outta here," added the red-splotched dwarf who returned carrying an armful of dead squirrels that smelled something awful.

One by one, he tossed the squirrels into the spaces between the slats, and Clifton grimaced at the crunch of bones and slurping sounds the animal made. "What is he...uh, Dalestrom, exactly?" he asked.

"*She*," the first dwarf corrected in offense, "is a pard, one of the most beautiful creatures you'll ever see. Mother of the leopard. Ya have that animal where you come from, dontcha?" Clifton nodded. "Then why ya wasting me time asking so many questions?" The dwarf's face turned beet red with anger, and now he looked more like the second one, who wiped squirrel off his hands and onto his shirt. "Let's keep moving. We're almost to the chimera."

Clifton gulped as the dwarves tugged him forward. "Out of curiosity, aren't chimeras, you know, dangerous?"

"All animals be dangerous," said the second dwarf, "if'n yer a danger to them."

The three moved in silence after that, and Clifton's heart raced in his chest. He knew of the chimera, the three-headed monster from Greek mythology with a lion's head, a goat's body, and a serpent's tail. None of that sounded good to him. What did it eat? And more importantly when it had last eaten?

A large building stood at the apex to the others and inside the darkness shaded the chimera. The dwarves stopped before the gate and untied Clifton's hands. He rubbed where the twine had burned his wrists. "Thank you," he said.

The dwarves ignored him as one moved to the gate lock and the other removed a metal triangle from a hook on the outer wall. Using a wooden stick, he struck the metal to produce pings and tings so soft, it sounded like Christmas bells.

"Why are you doing that?" he asked the skinny, splotch-faced dwarf.

A thud drew their attention to the gate, where the first dwarf laid flat on his face.

"Thurdamore?" the dwarf called, setting the chime back on the hook. He stepped toward the unconscious Thurdamore, leaned over his body, and was about to check his breathing when his own hand shot up to his neck. “What in the blazes?” He pulled something out and looked at it. “Not…good,” he said, before passing out on top of Thurdamore.

They were under attack.

Clifton searched for both cover and the culprit. The clap of hoofs on hard soil turned him around to face two pegasus ponies ridden by Dane and Liv.

“Yer welcome,” Dane said, as he put away his weapon and dismounted.

He’d shot both of the dwarves, like he had the guards at Droffilc Tower in England. Or like he *would* in 1485. Man, time travel could be so confusing.

“Are ya all right, Clifton?” Liv asked. “Did they hurt ya?”

“I’m okay. How did you guys get out?”

Dane motioned toward Liv. “Gifted pythoness, remember? When she recalls the spells at least.”

Liv smiled a tiny sideways grin to which Dane smiled back. “Let’s just say they’ll be sleeping for a bit longer than hibernation.”

“Now what?” Clifton asked.

“Now we go back home, boy. This mission of yers has ended. It’s over.”

“What? How can you say that?”

Dane prodded his pegasus closer. “Me pater is on his way to take care of yer arrows. Ya don’t need to be on this journey any longer. The stakes have risen, and the players have changed. Yer outta yer place, boy. Let the warriors take over from here.”

“You’re wrong, Dane. You might be afraid, but I’m not.”

"I'm not afraid."

"Prove it. Those arrows chose me for a reason, and you and Liv are part of that reason. We have to do this together or it will fail. Now, we have two reasons to help Robin and get back the Arrows of Light. No offense, but they don't belong to your father or your people. They may have at one time, but those arrows belong to no one. They choose who they are loyal to."

"Aye," Liv said, her stern gaze upon him. "And those arrows have chosen *you*."

Chapter Twenty-nine
The Chimera

Clifton inched toward the stable that held the chimera. In his right hand, he held a dead squirrel. In his left, a length of rope. "You sure about this?" he asked.

Liv nodded. "On three, Dane will open the gate and that chimera will charge at ya, understand? Dontcha be thinking he won't. As fast as lightnin', throw the squirrel high into the air as a distraction, so he'll need to stretch to reach it. When his eyes are averted, you wrap the rope around the lion and goat heads. And be quick about it. Once the serpent tail catches on, it'll swipe ya off yer feet."

He cracked his neck. "You make it sound so simple."

"Cause it is simple," Dane grunted.

"Easy for you to say. You just have to open a gate. I have to do everything else."

Dane harrumphed. "Ya know I've more ta do than that, boy. I'll be under its blasted belly helping ya do yer job."

"For heavens' sake," Liv said. "All the lot of ya have ta do is hold the beast long enough for me to cast the spell. Then he'll be like a kitten under yer command."

"Ya do remember this one, dontcha?" Dane asked, his voice tinged by nerve.

"Mostly," Liv answered. "Clifton, ya ready?"

"I guess," he said with a shrug.

"Mostly?" Dane echoed.

"On three," Liv continued. "One, two, three!"

With a shake of his head, Dane unlatched the gate and swung it open. At first, nothing happened, but then in a swift motion that spread over a few seconds, the great lion-headed chimera stepped out on padded paws. Its muscular shoulders shifted with each step into the moonlight, crimson eyes hungry. Fight or flight fear kicked is as Clifton launched the dead squirrel into the air. Just as Liv predicted, the beast lifted its eyes and bounded up on hind legs to reach the tender morsel. Clifton tossed the rope over the creature's neck and Dane grabbed the other end. The two crisscrossed in front of the monster, secured the lion and goat head, tightened the rope, and pinched the chimera into submission. The serpent-headed tail waved wildly. The goat head bleated in pain. Sickle-like claws dug firmly into the ground as the lion growled its displeasure.

Dane and Clifton held fast to the chimera as it fought for freedom. Clifton's arms grew tired from the monster's strength. Then, Dane was lifted into the air, as the chimera turned its great lion head, roared, and bared vicious teeth stained pink with the squirrel's blood. Clifton dug his heels into the dirt, but the rope whipped him back as Dane lost hold, flew through the air, and landed with a thud.

The chimera was free.

Liv stood before the chimera and said, "Submissionem ut Clifton Chase!"

The chimera stopped its fight. The serpent-headed tail surrendered. The beast softened.

"It's all right, love. Ya can let go now."

Clifton dropped the slackened rope, burning hands red from friction.

Dane stood and wiped dirt off his pants. "Took ya long enough."

"Can't rush spells. Ya know what happens when ya force magic."

The chimera sat on its haunches. It lifted a paw, licked it with a sandpaper tongue, and cleaned itself, tame as a housecat.

Liv scooted Clifton from behind. "Go on, now. Say somethin' to it."

"Say what? Hello, nice to meet you?"

"Dear God, lad, just tell the beast who ya are and where ya want to go."

Clifton gulped hard, stepped forward, and said, "Uh, hi." He turned for direction. Liv smiled warmly. Dane shook his head at Clifton's incompetency. Clifton faced the chimera. "Um...good, kitty?" The lion's gaze fell upon him and he head-butted Clifton, pushed him back, and resonated a low buzz. "Is he... purring?"

Liv laughed and pet the lion's head. "Sure is. He's tamed for now."

"What do you mean, for now?"

The chimera flopped onto its back, and Liv scratched its belly. "The spell only lasts awhile."

Clifton's eyes widened. "How long is awhile?"

"Don't know." The chimera's back leg twitched as Liv scratched. "Can't judge one by them all. It all depends on this creature. No telling, really. Perhaps a good solid hour. Perhaps more."

"Then it's best we be going," Dane said, as he tentatively touched the chimera's soft fur, then tied a square knot in the rope around its neck.

"I think yer right, dwarf." She moved so the chimera could stand, shake its fur back into place, and wait for direction. "Clifton, tell 'im what we need ta do and be polite about it."

"He'll understand me?"

Liv nodded.

He faced the chimera, still uncomfortable commanding such a powerful creature. "Mr. Chimera, we need to fly to Nottingham. May we ride on your back?"

The chimera lowered itself to allow Clifton to climb onboard. The creature stood and Clifton wobbled. He gripped tight to the rope and caught his breath on the majestic beast, although the serpent and goat head quickly moved in to get a better look of him, to which he held his breath in terror.

Dane and Liv did not climb beside him. In fact, Dane disappeared as Liv scratched beneath the monster's chins, causing it to slowly sag to the side. The chimera's purr rocked beneath Clifton, who overcompensated against the creature's angled posture. Finally, Dane reappeared leading two pegasus ponies that he and Liv mounted.

"Are we ready ta go?" Liv asked.

"As ready as we'll ever be," Clifton added.

With a sideways smile, Dane said, "Then let's get goin' before this pussycat realizes he's actually a vicious monster."

"Thanks for that, Dane. Appreciate the reminder."

"My pleasure, lad."

And the three rose into the night sky where the cool air lifted them through the clouds and toward the stars on a mission to help Robin Hood. On a quest to retrieve the Arrows of Light. On a task to save the people of Nottingham.

Part Three:
Castle Rock

Chapter Thirty
Nottingham

On a rock promontory, known as Castle Rock, towered Nottingham Palace. The hilly base spilled into a crossing of the River Trent that flowed as a picture frame half the length of the property. Large segments of green grass, trees, and wild bushes rose within the stone border wall. A large field butted up to the fisted rock hand that supported the palace, and in the cool morning haze of sunrise, it already showed activity.

Dane led toward a lower landing outside the view of the guard tower. The magical creatures were tied to trees, and Liv produced straw out of thin air to feed them. Clifton wondered if she could also produce a cheeseburger with fries but didn't ask.

They climbed the angled stone, moist with moss and dew, keeping low and traveling quickly under the cover of mist the world provided. Clifton's heart raced as he grabbed the slickened rock, lifted to the next level, and pushed his feet into any foothold he could find. At the base of the tower wall, Dane, who led the trio, stopped, and put his plump hand into the air to tell Clifton and Liv to hold their position. With their backs against the wall, they waited as the voices of the guards drifted down.

“Shouldn’t be long now,” said a bright voice. “Prince John is in good spirits.”

“And why wouldn’t he be?” replied a second voice slightly lower pitched than the first.

“Because, Percival, the tournament is rigged. Prince John knows he has the infamous Arrows of Light in his quiver, arrows even more infamous than Robin of Loxley.”

Percival sniveled. “In some circles, perhaps.”

“Why, you’d be a fool to think Robin even stood a chance.”

“Are you calling me a fool, Theseus?”

Theseus let out a shaky breath. “It is not that I am calling you a fool, my friend. It is that Robin Hood is the best archer in the world, in *all* circles, and I don’t think it matters if he’s shooting an Arrow of Light or a twig from a spruce tree. He’s not one to be defeated.”

“And I don’t think your mind knows what your mouth speaks.” Percival’s voice lowered. “You know nothing of the arrows, *my friend.* They are of Simurgh’s power. Her feathers fuel their magic, and the wood, carved from the ancient Tree of Life, where Simurgh nested.”

Theseus paused, then fell into riotous laughter. “You believe that nonsense, do you? Oh...then I do find you a fool, Percival. For believing superstitions of a thing made of feather and wood."

Percival's anger rose as he said, "Then you think your own kingdom a land of fools. I'll be sure to pass that opinion along to the Prince and Sheriff of Nottingham."

Theseus's laughter died down. "You would not dare."

"Wouldn't I?"

Dane faced Liv and said, "Now's our chance. Ready yer weapon. Clifton, distract them."

"Do what?" Clifton said, but both Dane and Liv had scurried up closer to the guards, scaling the walls like they were floating. Knowing time was not on his side, Clifton looked up and loudly cleared his throat. Instantly, the arguing subsided, and two faces peered over the edge of the wall. "Good morning, sirs," Clifton said. "I seem to be lost."

Arrows notched in bows trained upon him from the guards.

"And in need of fresh pants," Clifton added.

"Who are you?" Percival said. "And how did you bypass the River Trent without our notice?"

"You see, fellows, that's the problem with arguing. You kind of lose sight of what's right beneath your nose." Clifton laughed at his own joke. Percival and Theseus did not. "Look, I don't mean any trouble. If you could just direct me back to the main highway, I'll be on my merry way."

"Not likely," said Theseus. "You wait right there while I..." His hand lifted to the side of his neck and he pulled it back, stared at what must have been blood, and fell out of Clifton's line of sight.

Percival took a second or two to realize a few things: that his fellow guard had been shot with some sort of tipped dart, that the boy below was a mere distraction, and that he was next. But none of this ever left his mouth because a second dart hit his neck and took him to the ground with a thud.

"All right, Clifton," Dane yelled. "Yer all clear."

"Well done," Liv added. "Yer a marvelous distraction."

"Thanks, I guess. Where are you guys?"

They appeared on the edge of the wall, a few feet from the guards, as if they'd been invisible, which they most likely had been, considering Liv's knowledge of spells.

"There's a path at the edge, just ta yer right," Liv said. "It'll take ya here."

"But be careful, lad. It won't be long before the guards miss their check-in and this whole place is filled with soldiers."

Chapter Thirty-one
Surprised

Clifton crept up the sidewinding path till he reached the external wall where Liv and Dane waited. They were on Nottingham grounds, but not yet through the portcullis and inner walls. Together, they crouched and sped through the lower bailey toward the gatehouse that led to the castle. The pebbled streets of town lay empty as shopkeepers and merchants still slept. Only the baker's lamps burned. Clifton noticed several alleys where peasants slept around embers that smoldered in firepits. He couldn't imagine life in this century homeless, hungry, and dirty all the time.

The three reached the outskirts of the gate. The fortified keep was guarded by several uniformed men in towers above the portcullis, the façade of brick and wood sculpted around heavy oak doors.

"Now what?" Clifton said, as he stared at the impenetrable entrance.

"There's always a way, love," Liv said. "Ya have to find the patience to see it or else it could pass ya by."

Clifton nodded, as Dane felt along the wall and door seeking any give. Liv stood guard, her poison-tipped dart at the ready.

"What should I do?" Clifton asked.

Liv removed the long narrow tube for shooting from her mouth. "Watch for the way, of course."

Clifton laced his hands behind his head and turned around. A wooden fence rail bordered the treaded dirt path that curved out of sight and away from the castle. To the east, the Trent River ran into the distance slimming to a pinpoint on the horizon. The westward view produced the castle wall, the open archery field, and trees that lined the expansive property. A weird sort of sound caught his attention from down the open path. Behind him, the phlegmy kick of Liv's forced breath through the narrow tube was followed by a quick thud as another guard went down. That sound preceded two more and then fell silent.

"I think I got them all," she said, beaming.

Dane had given up on the chance of a way in through the sealed gate and joined Liv. He said something about her aim, and she giggled, swatted him away, and smiled. Clifton smirked. They were actually starting to like each other. He knew the outcome of their friendship would eventually become marriage, but it was pretty cool to be there at the start. This, of course, reminded him of Dane's untimely end, his death on Bosworth Field, that Clifton could have reversed with the power of the Arrow of Light. He chose to let him die on the battlefield. He had to warn him. Somehow, give him a glimpse into his future to prevent it from happening.

The weird clicking grew intense along with a whirr that caused the trio to stare down the dirt pathway. The steady sound was familiar, like horse hooves, though the thud was out of place. Except if hooves hit dirt, they wouldn't clomp, they would thud. And the whirr could easily be the wooden wheels of a wagon...

"Hide!" Clifton said.

He, Liv, and Dane dipped beneath the path on the grassy embankment beneath the railing and beside Castle Rock, and not a second too soon. From around the bend, a wooden wagon appeared led by several mares. The driver halted at the gate, called up to an empty guard tower, and tsk-ed as he waited for entrance. Two small-framed men dressed in uniforms jumped out from behind the wagon and called up to the men in the tower to open the gate. No answer, which made perfect sense because Liv had knocked them out with the darts. But if they were found that way, the whole kingdom would be alerted, and a manhunt would ruin their chance of helping Robin Hood.

"You've got to do something," Clifton whispered to Liv. "If that gate doesn't open, we are in big trouble."

"What do ya want her to do, lad, pop it open with her mind?"

He shrugged. "Maybe with magic?"

"Dontcha be thinking she'd have done that by now if'n she could?"

Liv was quiet as they argued. Her eyes squinted. Her lips trembled as she moved them. Her hands lifted and lowered, like she was trying to remember the words to a spell. "Ah!" she said, eyes wide and focused. She stretched her hand into the air, and said firmly, "Somnum ex vivifica."

Clifton looked to the solid wood doors, but they remained latched. What had that spell done? He didn't need to wait long for an answer. Above the gate, the guards' groans drifted down. She'd awakened them. "Good move," Clifton told Liv.

She smiled her reply.

The small-framed man called up again. "I say, good sirs, why are you not alert to post?"

A guard looked over the edge, his face pained. His hand ruffled his hair as if he rubbed a knot on the back of his head. "Who goes there?"

"Sir Monchat and the Royal Guards. We request the guard gate be opened."

"Password?"

He cleared his throat, as if a Shakespearean actor about to deliver his lines. "Benjamin gives needy dog to Ryan."

Clifton stifled a laugh. What kind of ridiculous—

The wheel above turned, and the gate doors opened.

"Many thanks," said the servant who returned to his position as the entourage entered the grounds of Nottingham Palace.

"Once they're through, we get up and inside before that gate closes," Dane said.

Clifton and Liv nodded, and the three pulled up as the carriage passed. The side doors had small holes to vent the air covered by privacy curtains. A second rectangular coach attached to the main cab had no windows on the side. As it passed, the opened back revealed its purpose. A prison cabin, with heavy metal bars to keep its captive locked inside.

And Clifton made eye contact with the prisoner. It was Robin Hood.

Chapter Thirty-two Shadows

Liv quickly handed Clifton and Dane a small bag. "Here. Cover yer temples and wrists with this."

Clifton dipped his hand into the bag. A fine powder stuck to his fingertips shimmering silver and he rubbed it into his temples. It cooled then burned, like a medicine for sore muscles. He touched more to each wrist. A wave pulsed out from each epicenter of powder on his skin, then faded. In fact, it kept fading, taking away the color of his skin, then his wrists and hands completely, and continuing its climb as it spread in warmth up his disappearing arms. His torso and chest were the next to go, followed by his lower body, legs, and finally his feet. He was gone, absorbed by the silver, able to see through himself to the ground. As it spread, he witnessed the affects the powder had upon Dane and Liv. They were turning invisible too.

Once cloaked, they moved in behind the carriage barely entering the grounds before the wooden doors closed and locked tight. It was difficult to move, like when closing one's eyes and attempting to feed oneself. He knew where his feet met the ground, but he stepped too hard and lifted too high, like he wore weighted boots.

"Stick close," Liv whispered out of nothingness. Her voice made Clifton jump.

"How?" he asked. "I can't see either of you."

"Kinda the point, dontcha think, lad?" Dane answered.

"Not helpful."

"Here," Liv said. A leaf lifted from the ground, floated toward him, and stopped. "Reach out yer hand and take this. Dwarf do the same. Place a leaf in yer hand. It won't be noticeable to anyone else, like a strong breeze passing by and nothin' more. But at least we'll be able to see each other."

"That's good, Liv," Dane said, as he picked up a leaf.

"Why thank ya, Dane. I do come up with some good ideas every nar and then."

"Aye, ya do more often than not."

The carriage drifted off the main walkway as the trio followed behind. Nervously, Clifton moved his leaf as if it really were caught in a breeze to avoid suspicion, although unfortunately, there was no breeze to be found, so everyone he passed tended to look his way.

"Put that blasted thing down, ya fool," Dane said. "Yer gonna get us caught."

"Sorry. I've never been invisible before."

"Well the whole point is to be unseen, since ya obviously missed it. Yer carrying on like yer the dang North Wind."

"Hurry up, ya two. The carriage is gone."

Liv and Dane's leaves picked up momentum, and Clifton sped up to match, careful to avoid a large pile of horse manure in the roadway. Jeesh. Imagine if he'd stepped in that. An invisible poop footprint running through Nottingham. He laughed to himself and hurried along.

At a fork that branched off toward a small building, sat the abandoned carriage. It no longer held Robin Hood. Clifton followed the leaves past the wagon and toward the front door, where he stopped short as the air knocked out of him and Dane grunted.

"Ya really are trying to give us away, aintcha?" Dane said.

"I'm sorry," Clifton replied, willing his breath back into his lungs. "I didn't realize you'd stopped."

"Can't very well open the door and walk inside. They'd think the place haunted."

Clifton smiled. "What's wrong with that?"

"Come again?" Dane asked.

"What's wrong with flinging the door opened and rushing in like a bunch of ghosts. They'd clear the room so fast we'd be able to grab Robin Hood without any trouble."

"Brilliant, Clifton," Liv said.

Dane scoffed. "Was my idea first."

"Aye, Dwarf, but the boy made it a plan. Now, on three, we go. Ready?" Liv didn't wait for their answer. "One, two, three!"

Dane and Liv pushed the door opened and it slammed into the stone wall with a loud bang. The guards whipped around to face an empty doorway. Clifton observed the room. It was a prison. Robin Hood had already been placed into his cell, and the guards were about to lock it when they'd barged in. This was their chance. Like Casper, Clifton oohed and grunted ghostly banters, his voice trembling with vibrato and volume as he slipped closer to the guards. Dane and Liv followed suit and the guards stared at one another, said not a word, and bolted out of the cell screaming.

Robin Hood's face was ash white with fear, but he saw his opportunity and started to run.

"Not so fast," Dane said, blocking him.

Robin jumped back into the cell. "Who are you, spirit?"

"The ghost of Gregory the Great," Dane said, "here to reclaim the—" Dane heaved as Liv must have gut punched him.

"Robin of Loxley, dontcha be fearin'," Liv said. "We're the three travelers ya locked in yer encampment."

"The dwarves?"

"Aye. And the boy, sir, Clifton Chase of the Park in Wickham."

Robin stared at the void, as if deciding whether or not to believe this explanation, before he finally said, "Show yourselves."

"As ya wish," Liv said. "Revelare."

In an instant, the invisibility ripped off like a bandage, and the three returned to full HD color.

Satisfied, Robin said, “How’d you escape my camp?”

“Me clan,” Dane said. “Attacked and killed many of yer men.”

“Why I am not surprised?” Robin said.

“They were only trying to rescue their loved ones,” Clifton defended. “Wouldn’t you have done the same? Your men attacked first.”

Dane’s hands balled into fists. “We’ve risked our lives and our pride ta save ya, ya ungrateful buffoon. The least ya can do is show respect.”

“Respect?” Robin belly laughed. “You want me to respect *you*? A sub-creature? A rebel and destroyer of my people?” He shook his head. “I’m sorry, my friend. You have wasted your time and made this trip for no reason. Now, you’ll kindly pass so I can get out of here and find my men.”

A battle cry caught their attention. From the opened door, Clifton and the others had an unobstructed view of the legion of dwarves that had infiltrated Nottingham. Torches ablaze, they rode through the streets, taking out soldiers one by one.

“We’ve got to get you out of here,” Clifton said to Robin Hood.

Only it was too late. A large dwarf spotted them and led a small squad toward the cell, with Drathco in tow.

Liv faced Clifton. “We will handle him. Ya must hide.”

“I can’t hide. I’m a part of this.”

Liv took his hand. “If we’re all captured, who will be left to rescue us?” Her soft smile carried her earnest message. Clifton nodded and Liv said, "Walker umbra."

"What does that do?" he asked.

"Stand in a shadow."

He did, and when his body entered the space, he felt a tug at his toes that spread up through his legs, his torso, all the way to his head as the shadow pulled him into its covering. Clifton hopped from shadow to shadow until he slipped outside the jail cell, past the advancing squad, and zipped around the back of the building, where instead of planning a way to help his friends escape, he sat down, covered his face, and wept.

Chapter Thirty-three
New Beginnings

The footfalls faded as his friends left, magnifying the roar of his cowardice. Although Liv had told him to leave, to plan an escape, to help them, he had left willingly, without so much as a fight. He had wanted to go. He had hoped to leave. Just like Ryan Rivales said, Clifton was fast to face his enemy only when he knew someone would be there to bail him out. And facing an army of dwarves didn't leave much room for rescue.

He cupped his head in his hands. Oh, why had he let Hobbie take those arrows from him in the first place? He could've fought him, that scrawny elf, and he could've found a way to hide them. But hindsight is never far-sighted, and this sort of thinking would not help him, his friends, or Robin Hood.

Or would it?

Simurgh made it noticeably clear to him that time was not linear when you moved in and out of it, that it only moved forward when you were within its boundaries. Could he find a way to slip outside of Time's hold and escape to the night when Hobbie appeared in his closet to steal the Arrows of Light? Sure, he could.

But how?

The Arrows of Light had chosen him, and when he needed them most, he had been able to will them into his possession. Once when he was in the English Channel... no, that wasn't right, exactly…the arrows had found their own way back into his hand.

He wasn't in control of anything.

He wiped his face dry and peered around the corner into the darkness. Nothing. They had all been taken away. The only things he could see were shadows.

Shadows.

He could slip from shadow to shadow and follow his friends into the castle, grab the arrows, and make their escape. It sounded easy. Too easy. And he knew that adventures never fit into maps or plans. But at least, it was a starting point. A new beginning.

Clifton picked himself up and leapt from one shadow to the next, his breath in the open expanse of quiet night the only sound. As he hovered deeper into Nottingham, he caught sight of torchlight. This could be bad, as the light would scatter the shadows. Yet that would also make more, which could be good. With no other plan, he continued on, sliding closer to the light and closer to the group of dwarves led by Drathco.

Dark voices grumbled as Drathco berated Liv and Dane for their actions, holding Dane accountable for most of it.

"And," Drathco continued, "ya let that boy into our home. Ya knew he had the Arrows of Light, yet he ate me bread and drank me drink."

"He didn't have the arrows on him, for the hundredth time, Pater," Dane hollered back, his hands unbound, surrounded by guards. "He came to me to help him because he said I'd helped him before."

The group of dwarves laughed. A snaggle-toothed one wearing a green frock said, "From the future, eh?" And the crowd erupted into laughter.

"Why ain't he more proper then?" said a black-haired dwarf with a beard that swept the floor. "You'd think being from the future he'd be better suited and taller. Smarter, even."

Clifton couldn't believe his ears. Why was he the butt of the joke?

"He is smarter," Liv said. "He outsmarted all of ya."

That quieted the group.

Clifton swallowed hard, hoping the sound would soak into the shadow that held him. Liv must've noticed, being the one who'd cast the spell that cloaked him, because her head whipped in his direction and he swore she stared right at him.

"In fact," she said, facing the order of dwarves. "He's probably already called upon the arrow thief since the Arrows of Light were in his hold, demanded his aid or his death." She faced Clifton. Now he knew she could see him. "He's probably called upon that wretched hob, as the Arrows of Light cannot be taken, only given away."

Clifton backed up until he rounded the corner. The fighting swelled as the dwarves continued to bark at one another, but the message to Clifton was clear. Liv was right. The arrows couldn't be stolen, not properly anyway, without leaving a connection from the owner to the thief, which in this case connected Clifton to Prince John. But holding that line together was none other than Hobbie. He was the one that took the arrows, but since he no longer had them, he was the one that Clifton could call upon for restoration.

Clifton ran back to the stable, hid in the shadows, and took a deep breath. "Hobbie, this is Clifton Chase. You stole my arrows, and I command you to appear."

Nothing happened. Only black night and grayed out trees had heard him.

"Well, it was worth a try," Clifton mumbled.

"What was worth a try?"

With a shudder, Clifton fell out of the shadow, breaking the spell. Standing before him was Hobbie. "It's you. It worked. I can't believe it..." Clifton stood, cleared his throat, and poised himself as if prepared to give a speech. "I am Clifton Chase and you have stolen my arrows. I demand their return or else... or else...."

"Or else what, sir?"

"Or else, I'll feed you to my chimera, who should be waking up right about now."

Hobbie fell to his face. "Oh, please don't hurt Hobbie, Clifton Chase. Hobbie was only obeying orders to the Sheriff of Nottingham. Hobbie would have been killed if he had disobeyed."

"Well, Hobbie still might be harmed by Clifton Chase," Clifton said, with no intention of following through on his bluff.

Hobbie looked up. His enormous green eyes watered and spilled over his bony cheeks. "Please, sir, you mustn't hurt Hobbie."

"Why is that?"

Hobbie stood, blew his nose into a handkerchief, and said, "Now that the arrows have been delivered, the Sheriff has released Hobbie from his position stating that it was my foolishness that has brought on the dwarves."

Clifton folded his arms, not understanding the connection, still trying to look like the one in charge, as best he could manage.

"Hobbie is no longer required to serve only the Sheriff of Nottingham."

"So, you're free?"

"No. Hobbie is still bound to the Sheriff, but not loyal to only his wishes."

Clifton shook his head. "What are you trying to say, Hobbie?"

"That I am bound to the Arrows of Light and to Clifton Chase too. Hobbie feels terrible for what has happened, and didn't even want to steal your arrows, sir. Hobbie had to. Hobbie has caused great distress between the thrush, dwarves, and Clifton Chase."

Here, Hobbie fell into a loud wailing cry, to which Clifton rushed to his side and comforted him in the hopes that the creature would shut up, seeing as how sensitive it was. "Hobbie, you have to be quiet. The dwarves aren't far away, and they'll come back for us if you're too loud."

This, of course, sent the little creature into further bouts of crying, though he covered his own mouth to keep the sound in.

Finally, Clifton said, "Hobbie, enough." The startled creature stopped his tears, stared wide-eyed at Clifton waiting for more rebuke. "I'm not mad at you. And if you can help me aid Robin Hood, I will forgive you."

Hobbie's eyes brightened. "Oh, really, sir? You will forgive Hobbie?"

"Yes. But only if you help me get back the arrows and rescue Robin Hood."

Hobbie stood at attention. "Consider it done, Clifton Chase."

"Great," Clifton said, his mouth pulled up to one side in a half smile. "How?"

"Well, you see, Hobbie has not been full of truth. I am not a particularly good servant, though I am an excellent hobthrush."

Clifton looked over the tip of his nose. "That doesn't sound promising."

"No, it is. It is. You see, the Prince and Sheriff told me to steal the Arrow of Light from a boy in a faraway land, which is you, of course, and I did that, you see?" He smiled a grin that made Clifton cringe slightly. "What Hobbie did not tell anyone is that Hobbie found three Arrows of Light. And, if I am not mistaken, that is too many for the Prince to use at once."

Clifton half-smiled. "Wait a minute. Are you saying you didn't give all three to the Prince?" Hobbie shook his head. "Where are the extra two now?"

"Oh, those arrows are safe in my chamber."

"Hobbie, you're brilliant. Can you bring them to me?"

"Of course, Clifton Chase. Hobbie had done a bad thing, an awfully bad thing. But helping you and Sir Robin will make everything right again."

"Yes, Hobbie. It will."

"Wait here," Hobbie said, and he disappeared into thin air.

Clifton swelled with hope, though a nag at the back of his brain warned this could be a trick. What could the hobthrush gain by betrayal to his master? He guessed it could be as simple as this creature didn't want to be under the Prince's thumb any longer, and this was his way to escape. Or he could be as treacherous as Clifton believed him to be and this was one long, elaborate setup.

"Here you go," Hobbie said, as he appeared before him and thrust both arrows into Clifton's hand. "If Robin's skills best the master's then at least now they are equally matched in weaponry."

The night stilled as Clifton reached out to take back the Arrows of Light. He inspected them, tapped the bodkin tip, ran the feathered fletching between his fingers, and smoothed the wooden shaft carved from the Tree of Knowledge. It seemed like the real deal, but what could a boy from the twenty-first century know about magic and arrows? They looked as plain as any others...

"Trust him," a voice rumbled inside.

Simurgh?

He stared into the night sky, scanned for dark patches where the stars disappeared, eclipsed by her monstrous form, and found none. Clifton looked back to her shimmery feathers on the Arrows of Light and stared. She was out there, he knew, and she had her eyes on him. He would choose to trust this hob and these arrows.

Even if it killed him.

Chapter Thirty-four
Chosen

Clifton leapfrogged his way to the guards. The shadows still soaked and released him as he passed through, but he noticed his image began to creep outside the lines of his own reflection as he neared his friends. The dwarves had settled in groups, with Dane and Liv no longer reprimanded, but now held as prisoners, cuffed to one another. They whispered when no one watched, and Clifton bet Liv was planning some magical escape that would happen at any second.

Instead, a fleet of horses drew in from the palace in a whirl of wind and hooves and shouting. The King's guards quickly surrounded the dwarves, who didn't lower their weapons right away. Clifton stared from the safekeeping of a building. On one hand, he knew he had two of the Arrows of Light in his possession, their power harnessed and at his will.

On the other hand, he knew this only because a mischievous hobthrush had told him so.

Not a very promising hand.

A guard hopped off his horse, marched up to Liv, and gripped her arm hard. She screeched, said some things in a foreign language that Clifton assumed must be ancient dwarfish, known as *Khuzdul*, and the man withdrew his hand as if on fire. With his other arm, he backhanded her across the face, which knocked both Liv and Dane in a tumbled heap to the ground.

Drathco drew his sword. “How dare you strike a child, ya pig of a man.”

“What did you call me?” the guard asked in a nasally voice.

Drathco motioned to his fighting force. “Dozens of dwarves armed with battle scars from killing the likes of yer kind, and yer cowardice chooses the weakest among us?” He spat on the ground. “Before this day ends, my blade will taste yer blood.”

Tensions flared as the two armies continued to ruffle their feathers in show. Dane and Liv had sat up the best they could with their hands tied and leaned against a small stump. Dane checked Liv’s cheek and she filled with fire. Clifton knew it was now or never. He drew a deep breath and stepped out of the shadows.

“Who’s he?” one guard yelled, and a domino effect of weapons turned upon Clifton.

Clifton held his ground, unmoved. Drathco’s face bore a look of sheer surprise, whether at Clifton’s bravery or stupidity, the boy would never know. Liv eyed him expectantly while Dane looked over as if wondering what had taken him so blasted long. But

Clifton didn't focus on the men or the dwarves. He thought only of home. Of his family. Of the families of Sherwood Forest. They needed his voice to keep their own. The quiver on his back trembled as the power in the Arrows of Light spread through him like warm oil.

The main guard said, "You don't belong here, boy. This does not concern you. Get back to your quarters."

"You're right, I don't belong here. But I am here and I'm not going anywhere."

The main guard, with eyes like blue gems, demounted his horse and stomped over. "You best hold your tongue before the Prince cuts it off. I said go home."

Clifton stifled a laugh. "Ever been homesick, sir, of the place you grew up in? Ever smell something that triggers a memory so real you would swear you were back in that moment? Imagine having the chance to make things right by going back to fix whatever it was that went wrong the first time around. Wouldn't you face it in the eyes? Wouldn't it be worth risking your life for?"

They stared at him, all of them, from the dwarf clansmen to the soldiers. Even Drathco. Still, he continued. "I have the chance to make this right, sir. You tell Prince John that Clifton Chase is here to set things straight."

"Why don't you tell him yourself?" said the guard.

From the shadows, a horse clopped closer, carrying a man with dark hair bound by a crown embedded with dazzling jewels. A crimson cape draped his shoulders and extended over the body of his horse. He stopped before Clifton and stared down upon him.

Clifton gulped what remained of his courage and took a step back, praying the arrows' strength would sustain him.

"You wish to speak with me?" Prince John said, glowering over the tip of his pointed nose. "And who might you be?"

Clifton teetered between a bow and a curtsey before he composed himself and said, "Your Highness, I am Clifton Chase, a mere boy from a distant time and place."

"From where do you herald, Master Chase?"

"From, the.... uh, Park of Wickham, Sir."

Prince John swung his leg around the back of his horse to dismount. "I am not familiar with your territory."

Clifton side smiled. "It is very far from here, but I have journeyed to help my friends and Robin Hood."

Prince John unsheathed his sword and stuck the angled tip into Clifton's neck so fast, Clifton wondered if he were dead already. "You are an enemy of the crown," Prince John insisted. "And will join the other traitors here."

Guards moved in quickly and reached for Clifton, who pushed back and ripped one of the Arrows of Light from his quiver. The bodkin tip sliced through the air and the shaft glowed. The men quieted and stared upon the mystic arrow that most had never laid eyes upon.

Or so Clifton hoped. He was betting on a hobthrush's word, after all.

Prince John pointed a shaky finger. “Where did you get that?”

“From its creator, Simurgh.”

“You know Simurgh in person?” Prince John’s eyes filled with fear.

Clifton’s confidence swelled. “She is a friend of mine, and she has sent me here. I demand the immediate release of the dwarves and Robin of Loxley.”

Prince John narrowed his eyes. He stepped carefully closer to examine the arrow but did not touch it. Finally, he turned his back on Clifton and waved his hand in the air. “That is not my arrow. It is a fake. The Arrow of Light is safe in my possession.”

“The Arrow of Light chooses its possessor,” Clifton said, and he looked over at Dane who nodded. “It chose me. Then your hobthrush servant stole it from my closet.”

“Yes,” Prince John said as he faced Clifton. “And he brought it to my chambers, which means it is in my possession. So, you see—”

“I wasn’t finished.” The Prince glared at the interruption. Clifton continued, unfazed. “Since the Arrow of Light chose me, and not you or your servant, it isn’t yours to possess. I’ll say it again. I demand the release of my friends and Robin now.”

“We’ll see about this. Guards, bring me my thrush. Now.”

Hobbie was in the guard’s arms before they knew it, as he’d been watching from the sidelines the whole time. The thrush was pushed from behind and he hobbled over, head down, mumbling, “It is true, sire. Hobbie stole the arrow from Clifton Chase but

Hobbie gave it to Prince John, see, until Prince John banned Hobbie from the castle."

"What are you saying, Hobbie?" Prince John said impatiently.

Clifton quickly took control of the conversation, before Hobbie blew his bluff. "He's saying that only one of us holds the true Arrow of Light. And there's only one way to find out which is which."

"And how is that, boy?" Prince John asked. "Will you be calling upon your friend Simurgh for wisdom?"

Clifton shook his head. "I challenge you to an archery match. Robin Hood with my Arrow of Light against you and yours to see who holds the true arrow and who holds a fake."

Prince John's smile widened. "I accept. Terms?"

"If Robin wins, you release us. All of us."

"And when Robin loses," Prince John said. "You will both stand in the town square and be hanged for your crimes against the crown."

Chapter Thirty-five
Gilbert Whitehand

The guards led the dwarves into a section of the catacomb dungeon. Clifton, Robin Hood, and the Merry Men went in a completely different direction. The rock hewn walls sweat, and the dampness triggered a sneezing fit Clifton couldn't control. Men pressed past, obviously still in an age when sneezing meant you'd caught something that would probably kill you. Looking at the passing crew, he found it odd that none of their hands were tied. But when they reached the carved-out room that they had to duck to enter, the shackles hanging from the walls explained why.

One by one, in the rotten expanse of the palace dungeon, Clifton and the Merry Men had their hands and feet bound. The guards took pleasure in their task, especially when they tightened the reigns on Robin of Loxley "the Greatest Archer in the world," they jested.

Finished, the guards exited, leaving behind the stench of their once-a-week showers. Obviously deodorant hadn't been invented yet. The room fell quiet as shock replaced the reality of their situation: they were locked in for the night.

Clifton yanked against his shackles, knowing it would do no good, yet trying all the same. With the archery competition to be held the next morning, Clifton understood he'd failed. The arrows had chosen the wrong boy. History would be altered forever.

"Master, Chase," Robin said, his voice sickly cheery in the claustrophobic room. "Good job at the rescue, lad. Most impressive."

Was he being serious? What a jerk. "Excuse me for not knowing in advance that you would lock me up in your camp and try to figure this out on your own. How is this my fault anyway?"

"Well yer in 'ere, and we're in 'ere," said Much the Miller's son. "And a lovely time around it goes."

The men laughed to which Clifton recoiled. How could they find any of this funny? "You know," Clifton said, "for a historical figure who has been depicted as brave and kind, you really aren't at all like the stories say you are."

Robin smirked. "Stories have a way of growing outside the scope of truth. That, my boy, is what makes them stories, and not facts."

Clifton shook his head and was about to give Robin a piece of his mind when he heard a loud crash. It happened right outside the small hole that must have been a window in the stone door that separated one part of the dungeon from the rest.

"What was that?" Will Scarlet asked.

"You'll be sorry," a voice shouted from outside their cell. "Once Robin hears how you've treated me, he will slice you up and serve you on Prince John's very own banquet table."

The door opened and a lad was thrown inside by two guards. Dark hair fell out of his ponytail in long strands. He met the wall with his face, hit the stone floor hard, and when he opened his eyes, he raised to his elbows and said, "That's all you got?"

The guards lifted him by his arms and slapped the wrist and ankle shackles on his scrawny limbs. He started to laugh. "Well, Robin. Didn't know you was in here."

"Yes, Gilbert. Just hanging around, you know, with the men."

"I heard you was in a match with the Prince." The guards tightened the shackles and Gilbert winced. "That'll be enough, boys, don't you think? Lessen you want me to lose me hands and feet to escape."

"Just be quiet," said a heavy-set guard with hair that formed a perfect bowl shape around his head.

The guards sauntered off and Sir Much leaned toward Clifton until the boy looked at him. "Watch this," he said.

The guards gone, Gilbert contorted his arms and shoulders till a popping sound sent shivers down Clifton's spine. He slipped one hand from the shackle, then the other, and with a muted scream, popped his joints back into place.

Robin laughed. "Now what, you fool? Gonna break your feet at the ankles and nub away?"

"Now, Robin. You know me better than that." Gilbert reached his immensely flexible hand to the bottom of his bare foot where he plucked out a key from between his toes.

"Where'd you get that from?" Will asked.

"And how'd ya hold it there while you's throwing such a fit?" asked Little John.

As Gilbert unlocked his ankle restraints, he said, "You know that's why I throw such a fit. I'm regularly a calm and collected sorta fellow, right Robin?"

"Whatever you say, Gil, just get me out of these restraints."

"Sure thing."

Gilbert quickly sashayed over to Robin and unlocked the wrist and ankle braces. The heavy metal clanked on the hard stone. Gilbert worked his way around the room, unlocking all the merry men until he reached Clifton. "Well, now, who might you be?"

"I'm Clifton Chase. Who are you?"

"Who am I?" Gilbert feigned offense. "I am only the most infamous arch-man in this part of the world. Women swoon at my presence. Songs are sung in my honor. Young men desire to be of my likeness."

"Uh...no offense, but it sounds like you're talking about Robin Hood."

Robin laughed so hard he could barely slap Gilbert on his shoulder. "See then, it's settled. My namesake carries through history much longer than yours, Gilbert Whitehand."

Gilbert pointed at Clifton. "The word of this boy is mere opinion, Robin, not fact. No one could know such things unless they were a sorcerer."

"Or a time-traveler," Clifton added with a tight-lipped smile.

Gilbert tilted his head, took in Clifton's appearance, and looked at Robin. He shook his head, then unlocked Clifton's shackles as well. As Clifton rubbed his wrists, Gilbert whacked him on the back and said, "It's nice to have a jester around for a change. These Merry Men can be so serious." He winked a sparkling blue eye at Clifton then moved over to Robin. "So, what's the plan?"

"Clifton tells of three Arrows of Light, two of which are in his quiver as we speak."

"May I?" Gilbert asked, reaching out a course palm.

Clifton looked to Robin for assurance, and said, "Sure." He handed one of the arrows to Gilbert, who turned it at every angle before giving it back. "It's a fake," he said. "Not the real Arrow of Light, I'm afraid."

"What?" Robin said, snatching the arrow from Clifton. "How can you tell? Looks perfectly well enough to me."

Clifton reached for the arrow, but Gilbert snatched it first. "Do you see right here, the way the light hits the tip?" The Merry Men craned their necks and grouped to get a closer look, squeezing Clifton out of the way. "That's how you can tell."

The men let out a unified sigh and moved away from the circle, leaving Gilbert sneering at Robin who stared at the arrow in sorrow.

Clifton caught the look on the man's face and said, "He's lying. You're lying!"

Gilbert zipped across the room and pinned Clifton to the wall. "Why would you say such a thing when we hardly know each other, especially after I showed you a kindness?"

"It's written all over your face," Clifton said, through restricted airways. "And I do know who you are. They passed down stories about you, too."

With that, Gilbert dropped Clifton and smoothed out his shirt. "Well, Robin, I think we should give this prophet a listen. Do tell, then lad, of my great legacy that spans through time."

"Happily. The stories I've heard all marvel about how Gilbert with the White Hand is *almost* as good as Robin of Loxley, in every…possible…way."

"Why you lying son of a—"

"Enough, Gilbert. I side with the lad," said Robin smiling. "You are always trying to outdo my efforts, and, in this case, I choose to trust that this boy has gifted me with the authentic Arrow of Light."

"And if you'd let me finish," Clifton added, though the look on Gilbert's face scared him half to death, "you'd understand that no other man in history can brag of coming close to beating the great Robin Hood, not in a single legend or lore I've ever read." Clifton produced the second arrow from his quiver and held it out to Gilbert.

Gilbert's eyes widened, then he composed his emotions and took the arrow. "I suppose it is hard to say whether or not it's a true or a fake. I, too, will choose to side with you, boy, and believe these are the Arrows of Light for which you speak."

"What's the plan, then?" asked Little John.

"Ask the boy," said Robin. "He seems to be running things."

The group faced Clifton, in search of answers that he didn't know if he even had. "Well," he mumbled. "It seems there will be a match tomorrow and it's really important that you win, Robin. I guess now that you and Prince John both have an Arrow of Light you're at least even at the start. We all know you're a much better archer, so it shouldn't be a problem for you to win now.

"And for you, Gilbert, you can be the standby in case anything happens. You are still a much better archer than the Prince, so it makes sense that you should hold the second arrow."

"That be a fine plan," Liv said, her voice muted through the wall.

"Liv? You can hear me?" Clifton said. "Where are you?"

"The whole blasted dungeon can hear ya, boy," added Dane, "flapping your trap like no one's listening. Gonna be the death of me."

A shudder swept through Clifton. Dane had no idea how close to the truth he was. Clifton would warn him that he would die on the battlefield in 1485. The thought crept back in, but he still didn't know how.

"Who is beyond this wall?" Gilbert asked.

"Just the dwarves that started the whole mess," Will said.

"*We* started it?" Drathco's voice rumbled. "You had better be glad there's a wall separating us, fool."

"This ain't helping none," said Liv. "We're all trapped in the same way, which puts us on the same side, whether we like it or not." The room quieted as she spoke. "The problem I see ain't that Robin Hood's the better archer, it's that if both he and the Prince carry the Arrow of Light, who's to say any of them're the real thing? Are ya certain, Clifton, that the arrows ya hold are the ones from Simurgh?"

Clifton shrugged. He couldn't tell them that he'd placed his trust in a hobthrush, a mischievous creature who played tricks on man, and one who in particular had stolen the arrows from his bedroom. He wanted to believe him so bad, he didn't listen to his own common sense. What a fool he'd been for trusting Hobbie.

"Trust him," Simurgh whispered through the darkness.

Apparently only Clifton heard her because no one else reacted. Nodding firmly, he said, "I'm positive."

"There it is," Robin said, throwing his hands into the air. "Now, let's all get some rest. The morrow will come before we know it."

As best they could, the men settled down on the stone floor. Clifton faced his back to them, not wanting anyone to see the tears that rolled down his cheeks.

What none of them could see was the young guard who'd crept passed the cell and into the shadows, headed toward the castle to tell Prince John the entire plan he'd just overheard.

Chapter Thirty-six
The Tournament

Clifton opened his eyes to the shouts of guards. Gilbert smacked him in the cranium to "wake him up" though his smirk led Clifton to believe it was for pure sport. He sat up and rubbed his head. The guards led the Merry Men out of the room and instinctively, Clifton reached for his quiver. It was gone. He scanned the floor. The open room left no crevice to hide in. Both the quiver and its contents were missing.

"You won't be finding them," said a guard wearing a dark hood.

Clifton looked up with his best innocent expression, and said, "I'm not sure what you mean, sir."

"You know exactly what I mean. Misleading the Prince is high treason. You and the men will be taken to see him now."

"No one's duped the Prince, ya mindless scum," yelled Will Scarlett, hands tied behind his back. "He's just dumb enough to fall for a half truth when it's presented to him." The guard shoved Will hard in the back, and the man winced, doubling over in pain.

A monster of a guard yanked Clifton to his feet, pulling too tightly on his wrists. "Wait," Clifton said. "What about the dwarves? Where have you taken them?"

A frail-framed man in matching attire leaned on a cane by the door. "They've already faced Prince John. Best be worried about your own hide."

The guards led out the Merry Men with Robin Hood and Clifton bringing up the rear. Robin leaned over and whispered, "Is this part of your master plan, too?"

Clifton didn't respond to his snark.

"I didn't think so. No matter, and in all seriousness, we will find a way to take what is ours and be victorious. The people of Sherwood are counting on me to keep them safe, and I cannot do that in prison or from a grave, now can I?"

Clifton eyed the man and for the first time, saw a glimpse of the hero who would go down in history as the Great Robin Hood. "I'm sorry I lost the arrows, Robin. I didn't mean—"

"Enough," the guard with the cane said. "You two pipe down."

"Of course, Bradford," said Robin. "Wouldn't want you to overdo it and fall like the last time you captured my men and I in the forest. I see you now lean upon a sturdy cane to hold yourself up."

The guard named Bradford grunted, then ignored Robin the rest of the way.

They marched through underground caverns in Castle Rock, up stone steps that led to a massive, wide-opened oak door. Sunshine spilled on the grassy archery field off the castle's edge flanked on three sides by a barrier wall of trees. A large wooden stadium had been erected overnight with long benches stretching the length of the field. Toward the center, a tall tower held Prince John and some lady with curled blonde hair parted down the middle and weaved with golden ribbons.

Maid Marion, he wondered?

At the base of the tower, the Sheriff of Nottingham stood guard with his men beside him. To the far end sat Dane and Liv, who held chained hands and whispered to each other, as Clifton neared. Drathco sat bound beside them.

What had Clifton done? What trouble had he gotten his friends into? He never should've trusted Hobbie, but the voice of Simurgh had been so real, so strong, so convincing. Had that been Hobbie's too?

The Merry men veered off to the opposite side of the field where they were chained together in a long line. The monster guard led Robin to the Sheriff. Clifton stood a few feet behind, sentries flanked on either side.

"Sheriff, it is never a pleasure to see you," said Robin.

"The same of you, Loxley."

"Ah, that's because I always outwit, outsmart, and outlook you."

The Sheriff stepped closer, his eyes twitching with fury. "Not this time."

"I am the handsomer of us, but we'll have to wait and see about—"

Before Robin could finish his sentence, the sentries yanked him to the platform before the Prince. One of them bent his hand till his wrist popped out of joint. The other smacked his hand with a wooden hammer. Robin's arm fell limp behind him, and when the guard's released, he hit his knees, wincing in pain.

Clifton flinched in sympathy. What had they done? Robin's bones had to be broken and if by some miracle they weren't, his wrist was most definitely sprained. No way he could shoot an arrow today.

From the top of the tower, a heinous laugh drifted down. "Not so talkative anymore, are you Robin of Loxley?"

Through the pain, Robin said, "Unlike you, Prince John, I do my own fighting and my own monologuing."

Prince John stood. "How dare you. When I win this competition, I will take great pleasure in watching you wither away in my dungeon. I think I'll enact a new tax, the Loxley Tax, and I'll take whatever is left from the people of Sherwood to pay for what you've done."

Robin smiled. "Ah, but that would require you to win first. And that's not going to happen."

"Your hand is useless. You are no longer a match for me." Prince John descended the tower ramp. "And I hold all three Arrows of Light, so I do believe I have an even greater advantage. Isn't that right, Hobbie?"

From behind the tower, a beaten and bruised Hobbie was thrust forward, bound at the wrists and ankles by chains that connected at the shackle around his neck. “The Prince is right.” He looked at Clifton. “Hobbie is sorry he let down Clifton Chase.”

Clifton nodded. “It’s all right, Hobbie.”

Prince John pointed at Clifton. “You’ll hold your tongue and not speak to my property.”

“Hobthrushs aren’t anyone’s property,” Clifton said. “Only the weak-minded bully those weaker than they are.”

Hobbie showed a grateful smile. Prince John glared.

“Would you have me destroy him now?” the Sheriff asked.

Prince John waved him away as he descended the side stairs of his tower. “You seem a brave lad. One who has gone through great lengths to protect his friends. It seems you might be well fit for me. What do you think, Clifton Chase?”

“You plan on breaking my hand first too, to make it a fair fight? It’s pathetic that the only way you can win is to take out your competition.”

“Very well, it is settled then.” Prince John stepped onto the field and said, “You will face me on the field in Robin’s stead. Only you will not be given any arrows from my kingdom.”

“What am I supposed to use then?”

“You have brought your own weapons, have you not?”

“You know I did. You took them. You took my arrows.”

"Me? No, Master Chase, I reclaimed arrows that were in my property. You and this hobthrush stole the Arrows of Light from my chambers."

"After you'd taken them from *my* closet first!"

"Tsk, tsk," the Prince said as his men slid on his chainmail and jacket. "I'm surprised you came all this way from another kingdom without so much as a dagger or a sheath. Guards, release his chains."

As the metal fell from his wrists, Clifton realized he had been snared by the Prince. He had no Arrows of Light, no weapons at all, and if he didn't hit closest to the bull's eye, they would all die. Clifton, the dwarves, the Merry Men, and Robin Hood. The people would have no protector.

And it was all Clifton's fault.

Why had he been brought there? What was it that Pearl had expected him to do? He was no match for this kingdom and no match for the Prince. He had failed. The arrow had chosen wrong and he had listened to a voice inside him that had been wrong also.

"Do you remember when we first met?"

Simurgh stood before him. They stood in a field by a lake, and the sun caught in her eyes and bounced off her hair. Her soft smile comforted him as he took in his surroundings. It was the forest between the dwarves' cottage and the town, Flaxton Village, where he'd met the two princes from his first journey through time.

"I told you that day the Arrow of Light would guide you and always serve you, unless you gave it away freely."

Clifton wanted nothing more but to bury himself in the soft down of her feathers, to take flight on her broad back and see the beauty of a world without borders and kingdoms and power. Instead, he stared up and tears filled his eyes, poured down his cheeks, and he collapsed to the grass. “I can’t,” he said. “It’s all my fault. I never should have let that hobthrush take them from me. And I never should have gotten my friends involved.”

“Good friends are involved by default,” Simurgh said, her voice a melody and harmony within itself. “Do you remember the gift the giants bestowed upon you?”

Clifton wiped his face and nose dry as he stood. “Yes. The Bow of Jehu.”

Simurgh smiled. “A strong bow that shot an arrow into a tyrant king, if I recall correctly.”

Clifton nodded. “But Jehu had arrows to shoot with. I don’t have anything. It’s hopeless.”

“Hope is an anchor that keeps dreamers from floating away. Hope is not what you need, Clifton.”

“It isn’t?”

Simurgh reached out her hand. Inside she offered the Bow of Jehu. “What you need is faith.”

As his hand clasped the bow, he found the ground pulled out from beneath him as the sky and clouds whirled into the mountaintops, sucked the lake up into a cyclone, and spat him out on the archery field of Castle Rock. No one else seemed to notice his absence, which was a particularly good thing.

“Well?” Prince John said. “What will it be, Clifton Chase? Are you ready to fight for your freedom?”

Clifton touched the wood of the Bow of Jehu strapped to his chest. It tingled, and he realized it was faith that he felt. He looked up at the Prince and said, “No. But I am ready to fight for theirs.” He pointed to the dwarf army, and to his friends, Liv and Dane. “And theirs.” Clifton motioned toward Robin Hood and the Merry Men.

“Seems an unfair trade,” Prince John said, “one life for the life of so many.”

“Not if you have nothing to lose. Not if you’re sure you hold the true Arrows of Light, and more importantly, not if you’re sure they are obedient to you.”

Prince John tilted his head in confusion. “What do you mean?”

“The arrows choose whom they serve, not the other way around. You might hold them, but that doesn’t mean you hold the power they possess.”

“Enough!” Prince John said, his face crimson with rage. “Let the tournament begin.”

“Am I supposed to shoot my bow without an arrow, really? You want your legacy to go down as the king who defeated an unarmed boy? Not very impressive, if you ask me, sire.”

Through gritted teeth, he said, “You will find an arrow from one of your friends. I am certain someone can supply your need.”

Clifton smirked. If the Prince only knew.

Prince John turned around and stomped across the field to the line marking the start. He lifted the first of the three Arrows of Light, inspected their authenticity to the best of his ability, and chose one to be his shot. Clifton could see that his words had power, and the Prince shook from the idea that he held the arrows but didn't possess their magic.

That left Clifton with a bow and no arrow. He faced Robin and the Merry Men. They had metal arrows forged in fire and bronze arrows detailed in gold. They were obviously stolen artifacts from the king's guard or collected from dead bodies after battle.

Clifton knew these were not the arrows for him. They could not be shot from his bow and they were from the Prince's kingdom. Eyes closed, he took in a deep breath, told his fear to calm and his muscles to relax. He thought of his purpose, his voice in the darkness as a light for those who could not shine. His friends, Dane and Liv, and Simurgh, with her purple eyes and glowing hair. He focused on the two princes he'd saved once before, Richard and Edward, from 1485, two boys who didn't stand a chance of success against a tyrant uncle, until Clifton was charged to save them. He envisioned Pearl, the beautiful Mergirl who had saved his life and was willing to sacrifice her own. Love surged in his heart for these new friends he had made along his journey's past.

He felt a tremble in his hand, as it rose, almost on its own bidding.

In his mind's eyes, he pictured Ava, her smooth skin and beautiful smile. And Justin, ribbing him for some dumb inside joke only the two of them shared. These were the people he was fighting for. These were the friends he would die for.

As the tremble in his hand grew to a shake, a power surged through him like a hot fire smolders in coal. His eyes opened. He stared at the arrows in Prince John's possession and focused on what was rightfully his. No more would tyrants bully those they perceived weaker. No longer would the *Prince Johns* and *Sheriffs of Nottingham* and *Ryan Rivales* rule the world with fear and fake power that they held over the heads of everyone around them.

Those were *his* arrows and he demanded their return.

The Arrows of Light began to glow. Prince John's face contorted as the shaft heated in his palm. It tugged away, by the look of his posture, and he held fast screeching for his guard's help.

Clifton's brow sweat as he focused on the arrows, thought of the sacrifice made for him by Dane, who would lose his life in 1485. Of Hobbie, who would lose his life most assuredly that very day, on Clifton's account. Anger and faith coursed through him. His hand heated as his body took on a strange glow, not dissimilar to the Arrows of Lift fighting to break free.

With a thunderous scream, the fletching sliced into Prince John's hand and as a swarm of bees, the three loosed arrows sprung to life and zipped through the air, only to land at Clifton's feet. He lifted one, placed it in the Bow of Jehu, and with a supernatural power he knew only Simurgh could have bestowed upon him, he spoke to the remaining arrows. On command, they lifted, coursed through the air, and found their marks in Liv and Dane's hands. The two dwarves touched the glowing shafts, and the golden hue spread around them as it had Clifton, knocking their shackles to the ground, and freeing his friends.

The two dwarves were immediately apprehended, but a quick spell fueled by the arrow's power sent them flying through the air into the tower that teetered from the impact. Standing beside Clifton, the three took on an ominous glow as they turned their Arrows of Light on Prince John and his kingdom.

The Prince held his bloodied hand as a servant wrapped it. His eyes grew mad. "You think your heresy brings fear in my heart?"

With a step forward, Clifton held his notched arrow in place, lined up with the Prince's target. Dane and Liv moved beside him, copied his stance. "No," Clifton said. "What you are afraid of is happening right in front of you. I will win this competition, and you will keep your word and release my friends."

Without a word spoken between them, Clifton, Dane, and Liv released. Their arrows flew through the air as free birds caught on a draft, speed and accuracy as welcome friends. Together, the Arrows of Light struck the bull's eye in one solid blow and as the glowing shafts collided, a sonic boom swept out from the target in a wave that knocked everyone to the ground except the three archers left standing.

Chapter Thirty-seven
United

Clifton stood dumfounded. He smiled from ear to ear, shocked and perplexed by the outcome. Liv turned to him, grabbed hold of Dane, and hugged them both for dear life.

"Ya did it, love," Liv said.

"No. *We* did it," Clifton answered.

The men and dwarves slowly recovered from the blow. Drathco wriggled his fingers in his ears as if trying to pop them. Little John rubbed the back of his neck. Gilbert Whitehand lay on his back and let out a hearty laugh, to which both Will Scarlett and Sir Much kicked him in the side.

Clifton saw his chance and stepped over Prince John, who sat coddling his wounded hand. "It's over, Prince John. You've lost. Now, let them go," Clifton demanded.

"Or what?"

"Or you'll go down in history as a man who did not keep his word."

"Only if you are alive to tell it." With a swift motion, Prince John reached into his coat and produced a dagger. His arm lifted to strike, but a flyaway arrow sliced past his nose, nearly nicking him, and he dropped the blade in outrage. "Who dare raises their weapon upon the throne?"

Hobbie held an empty bow that he slowly lowered. "I'm sorry, sire, but Hobbie said he would always help Clifton Chase, to make things right."

Prince John leapt to his feet, frantically pushing back his hair from his eyes. "This kingdom has gone mad. Where is the Sheriff?"

The Sheriff of Nottingham stepped alongside the Prince. "Here, sire."

"What took you so long? Never mind, now. Fix this at once."

"Fix what, sire?" the Sheriff asked, looking around at the men and dwarves scattered across Nottingham's lawn.

"This!" Prince John said, gesturing to the men and dwarves scattered across Nottingham's lawn. "Have you gone blind? Get rid of them. Now! Or I'll find someone more competent to take your place." He turned to leave. "And start with that hobthrush or he'll be the new Sheriff of Nottingham."

The Sheriff grew furious at the insult, his skin red and blotched with anger. "Men, these creatures are trespassing. Attack!"

Clifton realized the sound waves had ripped the shackles from the Merry Men's wrists. They now stood in a line, weapons at the ready. Weapons they'd definitely stolen from the royal soldiers by the collective look on the guard's faces. In a blink, the field filled with armed soldiers.

"It's about time," Gilbert said, smirking. "Hey, Robin, bet I can take out more guards." He climbed the tower where the Prince had been seated.

"Not probable. You can't possibly beat me," Robin said, poised to connect with the charging army.

"Why's that?" Gilbert called down.

"Cause you can't count that high."

Drathco and the dwarves clustered among the men. The brave creatures held razor sharp axes, pointy maces, and swords edged with diamond from the gems of their mountain. With Dane and Liv at the helm, Clifton filled with pride, watching as an army of men and dwarves put their differences aside to unite for one singular purpose: freedom.

Clifton took a step to join the army, when Hobbie tugged at his hand. "This is not why you are here, Clifton Chase. You are here for the Arrows of Light."

Reluctantly, Clifton agreed, knowing he was not a warrior, but a boy sent from the future to fix the past. He followed Hobbie's lead, out toward the target in the center of the field.

Robin Hood and his Merry Men collided with the Prince's guards. Robin seemed to dance his fight, with the light-footedness and grace history had told. Will fought hard. His sword sliced into the side of a solider, who fell to the ground. Gilbert Whitehand truly was *almost* as skilled an archer as Robin. His position in the tall tower gave him the advantage to take out several dozen soldiers with perfect aim and precision.

Axes raised, the dwarves took the open invitation to heart and swarmed the men of Nottingham. They used brute force and the pain from their past that had been miswritten, with Drathco spearheading the attack. His strength mighty, as he smashed his shield into the gut of a soldier, then struck another with the diamond-tipped blade of his axe.

Swords collided with swords. Shields blocked mace blows. Men and dwarf battled as one.

Clifton reached the target with Hobbie and fell to his knees. The Arrows of Light were mere broken shards of ordinary-looking wood that littered the grassy field. His heart grew heavy.

"Why do you feel sorrow?" Simurgh asked.

He was still on the field, though it had a glow to it, as if Simurgh had placed him in a bubble outside the grasp of any soldiers. "They're gone," Clifton said. "The last of the Arrows of Light are gone. What does that mean?"

She smiled. "It means, Clifton Chase, that the Arrows of Light chose wisely and died nobly. You have once again showed yourself a great friend and now, you no longer need the arrows. No one does."

"I don't understand. The Arrows of Light were supposed to be unbreakable, able to regenerate. What's changed?"

"Your love, Clifton. Your love for your friends and willingness to die in their stead has transferred the power from wood and feathers into the hearts of you, Dane, and Liv."

He took a step back. "Wait a minute. Are you saying that we're unbreakable?"

"Not in the way you may think. There is always a price to the magic, I'm afraid. And though it may seem great at first, there may come a time when the burden of the price is heavy. You are now connected to the Great Circle."

"The Great Circle? What's that?"

Her skin faded as the air took her away, the protective bubble evaporating with her final words, "You will learn from Pearl."

She was gone again, her voice an echo of confusion and peace like always. What had she meant about the Great Circle and the price of magic? He wasn't sure he wanted to find out.

When Clifton came to, the dwarves and Merry Men had the guards tied up in a large pile. Prince John and the Sheriff of Nottingham had been tied together, their mouths plugged with cloth to keep them quiet.

Robin Hood approached Clifton who stood to greet him. Clifton wasn't sure what to expect, with the look on the man's face, and as he neared, he braced for the worst. Instead, he was given Robin's outstretched hand.

"I owe you a great debt," Robin said. "We all do."

Clifton took Robin's hand and shook it. "I am honored to have helped you, and the people of Sherwood. And who can forget the Merry Men." He smiled. "Sometimes, your calling is given to you before you even understand what it is."

Robin side-smiled, eyes dancing. "I believe our calling is one in the same."

Clifton tilted his head. “You do? How?”

“Well,” Robin began as he paced toward the Merry Men, Will Scarlet beside him. “My calling is to be the voice for these people of Sherwood Forest alongside my men. We stand up to those who bully others and give the people hope. Is that not what you do, Clifton? Are you not the voice for those weaker than you?”

Clifton looked over to Hobbie, who wiped a tear from his eye. He shrugged. “I guess so, but it doesn’t feel so valiant as the stories I’ve read of you and your adventures.”

Robin clasped Clifton by the shoulder. “Stories are told so the truth can be heard.”

As he nodded, Clifton looked around at Dane and Liv, the dwarves, Hobbie, even the Merry Men, and realized together they had done exactly that. Together, they had turned the voice of many into something greater than any single one of them could have accomplished alone.

Hobbie stood beside Clifton. “Thank you, sir, for allowing me to make things right.”

“You’re welcome, Hobbie. What are you going to do with the Prince and his men?”

Hobbie smiled stained, crooked teeth and said, “Hobbie will give the dwarves and the humans time to escape before letting the Prince go.”

“Won’t he hurt you?”

“Oh, no,” Hobbie said, matter-of-factly. “Hobbie will leave to go back to his people. The Prince knows I can go and fetch the dwarf army now, so he won’t want Hobbie in his house anymore.”

Clifton smirked. “Nice job, Hobbie.”

"Yes, sir, but Clifton needs to leave now with his friends."

Hobbie moved back to where the men were tied on the field. From the woodlands, hobthrush poured out in droves, filled with mischievous laughter. Hobbie was going to be okay.

As he walked away, toward Liv and Dane, he thought about the Great Circle that Simurgh had mentioned, the one Pearl would explain to him. How would he find Pearl again?

"Well, lad, it seems we won," Dane said.

"Mostly because I was here," Liv added with a smile.

"Aye," Dane said. "Seems I won in more than one way." He kissed her hand and Liv blushed.

Clifton stepped back. "Uh, what happened here?"

"Oh, shut it, lad. You know exactly what happened."

"And," Liv said, "you know that Dane here will be me husband one day, dontcha?" She kissed Clifton on the cheek and bounced back over to the dwarf army to leave Clifton and Dane alone.

Clifton stared at Dane, who shrugged and said, "Can't fight the future."

Yes, you can, Clifton thought.

"Dane, there's something I need to tell you about the future. On the night that you and I fight King Richard III—"

"Come now, boy. You've told me enough already. Too much of ones' own future could be deadly."

"That's what I'm trying to tell you. It *is* deadly."

"Son!" Drathco yelled.

"Yes, Pater?"

Drathco and the army approached. Clifton tensed, but Drathco nodded his head and said, "You are a brave and wise human. Am grateful to ya for all you've done. Our kind won't forget ya in years to come. You and yer family will be under dwarf protective magic for the next millennia."

"Wow. Thank you, sir."

"Aye. It's the least we could offer. Now, men. We march back home with the Arrows of Light rightfully ours again."

"Oh, you can't," Clifton said. Drathco turned a displeased eye upon Clifton, and he wondered if the dwarf King took back all that protection talk. "What I mean is the arrows splintered when they collided. They're gone."

"Nothing's ever gone," Liv said. "Just takes on a new form, 'tis all. Like a spirit being reborn." She eyed Clifton as if she knew. That was part of Dane's death chant. What was she trying to tell him? Did she somehow know?

"Gather the splinters, men," Drathco shouted. "It's time to head home. Dane, Liv, ya stay behind with Clifton and make sure he finds his way home, too."

"Aye, Pater."

The dwarf army gathered the splinters into a cauldron by forcing a breeze to lift them up from the grass. Clifton watched them go, as Liv called upon the chimera to stand beside Hobbie and keep the men of

Nottingham from following any of them. Clifton waved good-bye to Hobbie, to the Merry Men, to the dwarf army, and to Robin Hood, who tilted his hat one final time before they all parted ways, never to cross paths again.

Dane led the way back through Nottingham, down the side of Castle Rock, and to the flowing water of the River Trent below. The rush of water filled their ears as they neared it and Clifton inhaled the sweet scent. As Dane crossed a rock path, Clifton tugged at Liv's sleeve. She turned.

"Liv," Clifton said. "I have to tell you something about Dane. I don't know how to, and don't even know if I should, but—"

She smiled. "I know something's been on yer mind about Dane since ya got here." Clifton nodded. "I wantcha to tell me."

Dane turned, but Liv lifted her hand. "Conglacior." And time froze.

Clifton looked at a fish who had only just hopped out of the cold water, caught midair like a photograph. "You really are an incredibly gifted pythoness," he said.

"Tell me of Dane. What is to become of him?"

Clifton took in a large breath, which struck him as weird since everything else had frozen. "When I meet you guys for the first time in the future, you are married, and Dane takes me to bring the Arrow of Light to the two princes it belongs to at that time." He stopped to pause, realizing the dwarves would be able to fix the arrows since he would get them again in the future…which was the past now. He shook his head at the predicament of timelines and continued. "We fight their uncle on a battlefield, much like today, only Dane isn't so lucky. It's my fault."

"What's your fault, love?"

Clifton's heart overflowed with shame. "He dies, Liv. Protecting me."

She took his hand. "Sounds like me Dane."

"But it doesn't have to be this way, does it? I mean, can't you warn him or say something? Use magic? I don't want to lose him if there's a way to stop this."

"Death comes ta us all, Clifton, as a welcome friend or a feared enemy."

"But he wouldn't have been on that field if I hadn't brought him there."

"I see." Liv pondered for a moment.

Clifton looked up to see a bird in midflight above him.

"I will promise you something. I will find a moment to warn Dane of what's to come, but I can't force him to do anything about it."

"You will? You'll tell him. Swear to me you'll tell him. Then he'll live."

"I swear it."

Live snapped her fingers, and the world flashed back to life, in a swirl of air and river and birds, and Dane's gruff voice as he said, "Clifton, I believe you and Pearl have met."

Chapter Thirty-eight
History Repeats

Pearl leaned her heart-shaped chin against her elbows on the riverbank. With a friendly smile, she said, “Hello, again.”

Clifton knelt to meet her gaze. “Hello, again to you.”

“So?” she asked. “What did you think?”

“About what?”

“About your adventure?” She flipped in a somersault, smacked her shimmering tail against the water, and splashed Clifton and the dwarves.

Bubbles surfaced and popped out laughter, and Clifton couldn’t help but laugh back.

Dane and Liv hovered off to the side, where Dane somehow managed to smoke a pipe, though Clifton wondered where in the world he’d kept it all that time. Liv held his hand, leaned her head upon his shoulder, and closed her eyes, a content smile on her lips.

Pearl was leaning against the bank again, captivating Clifton with her wide, blue eyes. "Are you ready now? To go home?"

Home.

He nodded. "Can I say good-bye to my friends first?"

"Of course, silly. I'll wait right here."

Dane blew out a ring of vanilla scented smoke as Clifton neared. He squinted from the high sun behind the boy and said, "You gonna be all right, lad?"

Overwhelmed with emotion, Clifton put his arms around the little man and scooped him into a tight bear hug. Dane squirmed—which ended up being a good thing because it made Clifton laugh instead of cry—and pushed him away. "Blasted, boy. Why are ya hugging on me?"

"I'm just really gonna miss you."

Dane relaxed and hugged Clifton back. They separated and he said, "I hope when we meet in the future, ya aren't so needy." Dane smiled his crooked little grin and tilted his hat down over his eyes. "So long, Clifton Chase."

Liv stood and pulled Clifton a step or two away from Dane's earshot. She hugged Clifton tight. "I will miss ya very much, Clifton." She took him by the hands and said, "Yer secret is mine and me heart is his." Then, she pressed two fingers into Clifton's temple and whispered, "I'm sorry to do this, but I don't wanchya spending yer life worried about Dane anymore."

"Huh?"

"Obliviscatur."

A lightning bolt pulsed from his head to his feet and Clifton stepped back. The edges of his vision went fuzzy. His eyes took in his surroundings as the dwarf led him back to the shore where a beautiful mergirl waited for him. He knew her, this mergirl, who took his hand and pulled him into the water to wade with him. Clifton peered over his shoulder where he saw two dwarves, like the kind from the storybooks he read as a child, smiling at him, waving good-bye. Clifton waved back, because he knew it was the polite thing to do, though he couldn't quite place who they were or why they seemed so familiar.

As the water reached his chest, he turned to face the mergirl. "What's your name?" he asked. "You're very pretty. Is this a dream?"

She smiled, as she attached something clear and gelatinous to his face to cover his mouth, eyes, and nose. Then, she dunked him under and a panic spread over him as the creature pulled him deeper into the water.

"Breathe," she whispered. "You will be okay."

Without another option, Clifton took in a deep breath and instead of water, air filled his lungs. He could see through the mask, as this beautiful mergirl pulled him deeper and deeper, away from... from what? Where had he been? He was supposed to ask her about something important. Something great…What was it? Why couldn't he remember anything?

The water swirled around him in glittery shades of blues, greens, purples, and reds, and he grew afraid as he suddenly realized he was alone in the deep. The being, which he couldn't remember now, who had brought him there, had disappeared, leaving him alone in the torrent of water that flung him around and upside-down until he could no longer tell his direction. Sound and light swooshed in and out.

He must have been dreaming, for this wasn't possible.

The pressure intensified as the world around him grew dark and silent. He wondered if he had died as everything stilled. But a small, pinprick of light caught his eye, and not knowing where he was or how he'd gotten there, he grew curious and swam toward it. The light lengthened into rippled waves as he drew near the surface, where he pushed out, took in a huge breath, and heaved himself up onto the shore.

Clifton rolled onto his back and caught his breath. He had no memory of where he was, how he'd arrived, or where he'd come from. He had a strange suspicion that someone had done something to him, but he couldn't remember what. Faintly, he heard his name being called. Clifton sat up, strained to listen. He heard it again.

"Dad?" Clifton yelled back.

"Clifton?" Dad answered. His feet pounded the packed dirt of the woods that surrounded Clifton and his voice carried through the branches until he came into sight. Clifton's dad knelt beside him. "What happened? Are you okay? Did you hurt yourself?"

Clifton stared into his dad's face and it was as if a fog lifted from his mind. Many things came back to him, including he and his father talking about a trip to Wickham Park to shoot arrows. "Are we in Wickham Park?" he asked.

Dad's face cloaked in worry. "We've got to get you home." He grabbed Clifton beneath his arms to lift him, but Clifton waved him off with a smile.

"Dad, I'm fine. Really." Dad didn't look convinced. "I must have fallen into the water."

"Why were you even near the water?"

Clifton shrugged. "I don't know, but I think everything is okay now, you know?"

Dad's smile curved at one edge. "You sure you're all right?"

Clifton stood up for proof. "I'm great, Dad. Except for grandpa's arrows going missing."

"Going missing? What are you talking about?"

Clifton's dad turned on his heels and bounded back to the archery field with Clifton right behind him. They crossed through the woods, where images of Robin Hood and his Merry Men clung to Clifton's mind like the tail end of a wonderful dream you don't want to wake from. The trees parted and opened to the field he knew so well. At one end stood a lone target. Leaned against the post, Clifton's quiver seemed to glow.

"Grandpa's arrows are in there," Dad said. "Go grab your stuff and I'll get the car."

Dad went to start the car and Clifton fetched his quiver. As he moved closer, he laid his eyes upon grandpa's arrows and gasped. A piece of his mind must have opened up because he remembered something.

It wasn't his quiver that was glowing.

The Arrows of Light had returned.

Book Two

To Be Continued…

Acknowledgments

A big thank you to everyone who has embraced Clifton Chase, shared him with a child, or invited me into their school to talk to their students about bullying. For Castle Rock, I'd like to thank my INCREDIBLE advanced readers who helped to perfect the book for publication:

Jessica Paolicelli
Clara DiBella
Angela Barnes
Carol Guchek
Lisa Irizarry
Jesse Hall
Elaine & Jason Irizarry
Candice Elkins & son
Keith Helton
Sarah Chang
Shrima Sridharan
Raymond Mojica Jr.

"Hope is an anchor that keeps dreamers from floating away. Hope is not what you need…what you need is faith." –Simurgh, the Bird of Reason

Bullying is a real issue, and you can help by remembering that your words have power! You can speak life into others by building them up or you can destroy them with what you say. Always remember the Golden Rule, and that sometimes, you must be the voice for someone who can't. Stand up by using your magic words to fight bullying!

If you enjoyed this book, please take a moment to review for other readers to discover it.

Become a fan @JaimieEngleAuthor

Want more? Become an Engledork, for freebies, fun & more!

About the Author

Jaimie Engle has been writing since she was seven years old. The idea for Clifton Chase was inspired by a real-life oil painting depicting the Battle of Bosworth Field, the same painting she included in Clifton's story. She lives in Florida, just near Wickham Park, with her husband, youngest son, and a hound dog. Visit www.JaimieEngle.com.

About the Illustrator

Debbie Waldorf Johnson worked over 25 years in graphic design and spent a few more years painting and teaching watercolor. She has won several awards for her watercolor paintings. As a grandmother, Debbie enjoys creating images for her grandchildren, picture books, and commercial publications. She lives near the ocean with her husband, Ken, in Melbourne, Florida, where they love getting a little sand between their toes. Follow her at Debbiejohnsonartist.wordpress.com.

Made in the USA
Columbia, SC
15 February 2021

32752961R00136